THE

# MACE

MYSTERY

*&*

OTHER
MUSINGS

THE

# MACE

MYSTERY

*&*

OTHER

MUSINGS

EMMA ADAIR

First published in 2025 by Adair Gallery
Copyright © Emma Adair 2025
The moral right of the author has been asserted

10 9 8 7 6 5 4 3 2 1

ISBN (Paperback) 978-0-6489399-3-1
ISBN (eBook) 978-0-6489399-7-9

A catalogue record for this
book is available from the
National Library of Australia

NATIONAL
LIBRARY
OF AUSTRALIA

Cover image terentyevner55 | Adobe Stock
Book design by Beau Lowenstern

*For people who are*
*suspicious of coincidence*

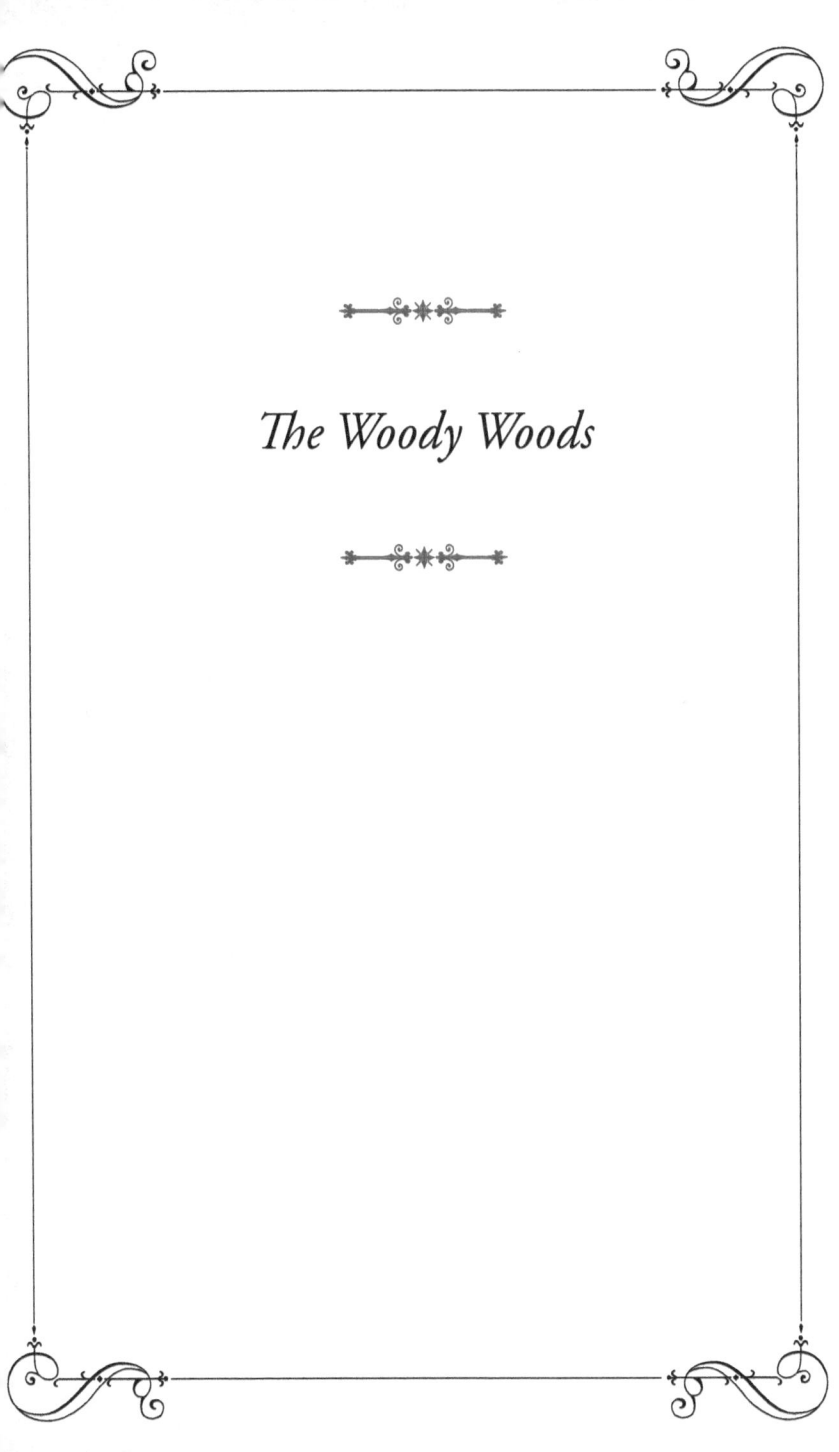

# The Woody Woods

A wretched man trod along a cobbled path. The woody woods towering above ignored him as he moped. Unsympathetic. Uninterested in his journey.

The man, tired of the trees, saw a parting ahead and quickened his pace. Eager for respite.

As the wretched man emerged in a clearing he realised there was a divergence. Opposite, there were two paths.

To the side of the fork a small person lay on a bench, curled like a snail. The person, startled by the man, briefly uncoiled and then swiftly recompressed. They tapped their hand on the seat, inviting him to sit.

The man, weary from his travels, did not wish to entertain a conversation but was aching to rest, and accepted nonetheless.

The person stirred, awakening from their slumber.

"Where are you headed, my friend?" the person asked the man groggily.

The wretched man was offended this stranger would be so bold as to call him friend but felt them unworthy of confrontation. "I am on my way to greener pastures."

"Hmmm," the person contemplated.

The wretched man now primed to converse was slighted at the dismissal. "Where are you headed?"

The person thought on the question and looked to the paths, hovering over the reply.

"I do not remember," they answered. "I have been here a long time."

*How absurd*, thought the man. "How long is a long time?"

The person, with an outstretched hand, reached for the truth invisible in the space in front of them. With nothing to grasp, they retracted.

"At least a thousand years," they offered in place of certainty.

The wretched man found it hard to believe but was unwilling to waste his precious curiosity on the stranger and nodded. His capacity to maintain offence had expired.

"What is wrong with the grass from whence you came?" Their creased cloak shivering with the weight of the words.

The question stabbed the man in the heart. The woody woods knew. Unworthy though this person may be, he felt honesty brewing on his tongue. "I was a wretched man."

The woody woods confirmed his story and the person nodded along with the leaves.

"So it is not the grass that is the problem," the person surmised.

The wretched man felt soaked in shame. "No, it was not the grass."

The person shuddered then straightened, dislodging ever more dust with every stretch.

The wretched man, desperate to evade the mirror, cast attention elsewhere. "Why have you waited here on this bench for a thousand years?"

The person thought they knew but could not be sure. "I expect, when I sat, I was trying to decide which path to take."

"You do not know?" the wretched man asked, disturbed by the thought of never leaving this bench.

"I do not know, I suspect," the person explained, eyes fixed on the cobbles.

The wretched man had not yet turned his mind to which path to choose. They looked identical. There was no way to know what was at the other end. He felt bad for the person, trapped in their indecision, and ashamed by his haste to judge. He did not want to be what he was, a wretched man.

"I am sorry. It is a very hard decision. I too cannot tell which is a better choice. The paths look the same," he replied, his gaze darting between the openings.

The person followed his stare to their conundrum.

"Now, even after a thousand years, they are each as compelling as they were the day before," the person remarked affectionately.

The wretched man was confounded by the person's contentment. A thousand years lost to this clearing. The wretched man swelled, full of amazement.

The person turned from the paths back to the wretched man. "Which path will lead you to grass where you will no longer be wretched?"

The man faced the miserable fact that he may be wretched everywhere but nonetheless was determined not to get stuck on the bench with the person forever.

The woody woods glared at him.

"It is not the grass, it is me. It is the wretchedness that I will leave behind. Whichever path I take, it will not matter," the man replied confidently.

The person chuckled. "If your wretchedness is so loose, why do you need to seek new grass?"

Frustrated, the man went to inspect the openings. Up close, they were still indecipherable. He pawed at the foliage, sniffed the pollen, stroked the petals. They were the same.

He returned to the bench.

The question burned. The breeze knew. The wretchedness was not so easy to shed. The grass from whence he came was fine grass.

"Do you think you will ever choose a path?" the man asked.

The person was enamoured with the possibility.

"I may very well do."

"You could walk one path and if you do not like what you find, walk back to the clearing and then take the other path."

The woody woods sighed.

The person considered the man's advice. "There would be two paths upon my return."

The wretched man understood. There were three paths.

The person contemplated leaving the clearing at all.

"If it helps, I know the grass at the end of this path is good, fine grass. This is a good path," the man said pointing to the path he had taken.

The person was amused by the recommendation. "Yet you would choose unknown grass over known fine grass. Are you wretched or a fool?"

The wretched man knew he was both wretched and a fool and instantly felt the pull of the path he knew, the good, sweet, known, fine grass.

"I am a wretched fool!" Unable to hide his shame from the woody woods, the man plunged his face into his hands.

"May I suggest, friend, that you leave your wretchedness on this bench and return down the path from whence you came, back to the grass you know. If it is, as you say, you, not the grass."

The woody woods smiled. The person smiled too.

"I do not want to leave my wretchedness here with you on this bench," the wretched man pleaded, fearful it would be a wretched act to do so.

"I will gladly absorb your wretchedness. It may help me choose a path," the person replied kindly.

The wretched man looked upon the grace of the person and felt the wretchedness lift and depart.

The wretchedness settled on the person, smoothing the ancient creases from their cloak.

The man stood. Unburdened by the transfer, he sprung up faster than he could before and stumbled a few steps back toward the sweetest known grass.

"Farewell, friend. Enjoy the grass," said the person.

"Thank you, friend. May your path reveal itself to you," the light, free man replied.

"You are most welcome." The person smiled and waved.

The man left.

The person winked to the woody woods and the leaves cheered. They looked to their paths and pondered their eternal hope, shrouded in their new wretchedness, willing the next thousand years.

# Poetry

# Two Birds

On a branch two birds sit
Sharing the same world
Some days together some apart
Always returning
No matter the space in between
The time since meeting uncounted
The next day certain
The world from the branch theirs
A single view together
No different to the world alone
Doubled however
Colours brighter
Smells sweeter
Sounds richer

# Fool Soup

In the space between certainty and uncertainty is a delicious valley. Overflowing with options. Enticing lingering camouflages stagnation. Greedy. The valley so easy to slide into, exhausting to climb out. Time wasted disguised as time spent. Distraction from the climb. Seducing promise hides stagnation. Delay dressed up as decision. Fuzzy indecision its allure. Dilution of purpose its secret. Thickness in the valley warm and deceptive. The razor of certainty beyond the crest a distant future. Beyond the climb. Meanwhile the valley of fools. Trapped forever in a soup of possibility.

# Love

A man is a man
Two legs, a face, a body, hands, hair
A thousand men are all still a man
A thousand heads
Yet there is only one head of a thousand heads
Why this one
What about this head is unlike the other heads
Everything
Nothing at all, they all have ears, a smile, a nose, eyes
Nothing is the same but everything is the same

# Bitter Women

Ability
Capacity Awareness Willingness
Temperament
Fear Identity Resignation
Possibility
Time Context Effort
Resentment

# Gods

Floating above, wasted and adored
Visible contrasted, ever illuminated
Muted and dulled
Existing, suspended, unroused

Rare alignment recalibrating
Instinct reawakened
Desire remembered
Reconnection sating

# Soul

As the crumpled soul lay resting in the snug embrace of
    the mind, it whimpered coarsely.
Little soul, said the mind, why are you so worn, such a
    little soul should not be so tired.
But I am so, said the soul.
Soul, you are still so small, and you have far to go,
    perhaps you are not tired but growing into a bigger soul.
Mind, you are so smart but I the soul am wise, my size
    you see is not why I am tired, but the road is long, and
    my small size will not grow.
But soul, if you are tired, you must grow.
Mind, it is the road which must grow not my size, a soul
    is always wise.
But soul, if you were wise, you would not be tired.
Mind, I am tired because I am wise.

# Effortless

Volume of obligation unshiftable
Fastened unbreakable as birth
Fibres stretched tense
Exhausted by the wait for hindsight
Like for like
Cancels the burden
Motives expired
You are effortless

# Land and Time

Why, land and time, are you conspiring to deceive me?
I beg you for air, and you give me smoke.
I thirst for a crisp blue sky, and you give me heat.
I long for the sweetness of touch, and you give me space.
I long for endless forest, and you give me dirt.
Withholding your fruits so cruelly.
Refusing my desires, you have my attention.
Angry world, I know you do not need me, but I need
    you.
Calm your skies and seas.
Remember how tenderly I care for you.
Give me your freedom again, land and time.

# Courage

Courage is action in the presence of fear. So what is action without fear? What better world could I create? A sale unlike any other. A sale with no price. No condition. No product. A product with no purpose. The sale of oneself. Cells ever changing. Instantly different. What a risk. Or to become the purchaser. Acquisitional pursuit. The sale of air or the purchase of air. The courage to sell air. The audacity to buy time. Stripped of possession. To share air and time. To give you my air and ask for your time.

# Life

The journey makes its mess,
the plan its own path.

The heart chooses its desire,
the magnet draws its match.

The beauty lingers in the stitching,
a life the squares in between.

# Trust

To trust without change is to neglect our everfoaming
nature.

An impossibility to trust without focus.

As we change, our trust can only equally change or be
lost.

How to trust every day, without renewal every day.

Searching for the shift and realigning.

All energy must first be dedicated to that search.

A connection formed upon which all else rests.

To be able to believe that bond is unbreakable without
investment.

Is a deceit, sloppy and cruel.

# April Fool

A day for fools
Only a single day
Such a long wait for relief of one's inhibitions
Alone, drifting among all other days
Desperate for release
Unleashing upon the sensible world
Terse and blissful
A moment to forget the grey of every other day

# Stunt Life

Plonked in the centre,
surrounded by stunts,
how does one awaken to a life,
constructed by other's hands?

Pretty at the centre,
dressed and draped for show,
a life for all to envy,
a life to call one's own.

# The Mace Mystery

This fictional story was inspired by the true story
*Who Stole the Mace?* by Raymond Wright

# 1

Tamzyn leant over a coffee table between two regal armchairs and stroked a velvet curtain. She turned to Michelle with a raised eyebrow. "I've heard Annie's girls spend their spare time volunteering?"

Before Michelle could answer, their hushed conversation was interrupted by a stunning woman in a suit. "Detectives, Annie will see you now."

Tamzyn followed Michelle. She'd never been inside Madam Brussels.

The office door was open. Annie sat at her desk reading a newspaper.

"It's lovely to see you, Michelle. You look well." Annie stood to greet her old friend.

"Likewise." Michelle valued her praise, Annie was the epitome of elegance.

Annie invited Tamzyn and Michelle to sit opposite her in high back chairs with gold frames.

Annie noticed Tamzyn's fleeting surprise at the breadth of mastheads fanned across her desk.

"A cultured woman must be apprised of all manner of topics," Annie chided and turned to Michelle. "And this is?"

"My partner. Detective Tamzyn Nixon."

Annie appeared unimpressed but accepted the stranger's presence in her inner sanctum. Annie trusted Michelle's judgement.

"I got your message. What happened? Are you and the girls alright?" Michelle asked. She had been worried. Annie hadn't reached out for help since Michelle had saved her from a stalker way back when she was a junior detective.

"We're all fine, but someone has been cutting our phone line. The first time it happened I thought perhaps it was a mistake, or an electrical fault, but this is the third attack. I don't want to make a formal complaint, I just want it to stop."

Famous and exclusive, her massage parlour's elite clientele relied on Annie's discretion.

"Do you know who it is?" Michelle asked. She knew Annie was aware the police couldn't solve a crime without an investigation.

"I assume it's the jokers over at Parliament."

One quick phone call and Annie's clients could make it back to Parliament in less than four minutes.

"I understand." Michelle masked her disbelief. Annie's world was awash with absurdities to which Annie was completely desensitised. "What do you need?"

"I suspect a quick chat with the doorman will suffice. Nothing more official is required."

Michelle suspected anything more official from Annie would not involve the police.

"No problem, if that's all you need," Michelle agreed.

"Thank you." Annie rose to accompany them out. "How's Tessa?"

"Good, stressed. She's just about to start her final exams. How are the girls?"

Annie didn't have children but treated her staff like daughters.

"A bit unsettled by these pranks, but otherwise well."

"We'll head over to Parliament now. Please call again if you feel unsafe," Michelle insisted. She didn't want Annie taking retribution into her own hands.

"Of course," Annie lied.

The detectives departed.

Tamzyn smirked. "Are we really off to Parliament?"

Michelle was unimpressed by her partner's amusement when Annie might be in danger again. "Yes. Really."

§

Michelle and Tamzyn skipped the queue and walked toward the public entrance into the parliament building.

"Sorry, ladies, no special treatment," a security guard bellowed from his post.

"I'm Senior Detective Ward and this is Detective Nixon. Are you in charge?" Michelle said bluntly and waited for the about-face. They didn't wear police uniforms.

"Apologies, Detectives. I'm just the doorman, Fredrick Davis." He stuck his hand out to greet Michelle. "What can we help you with today?"

"Someone cut the phone line at Madam Brussels. We thought because you're out here on the steps you may have noticed something suspicious," Tamzyn suggested casually.

Fredrick flinched at the name.

"I've never heard of Madam Brussels but I've not seen anything out of the ordinary. Of course, because I would have called you,"

Fredrick rambled nervously.

Madam Brussels was not visible from Fredrick's vantage point. He understood Tamzyn's implication.

"That's a shame because we have no leads at all. Oh well, we best keep moving. Thanks for your help, Fredrick," Tamzyn said, reading his name off his nametag.

Fredrick nodded and blushed.

Michelle gave Tamzyn a wink and they walked back down the steps.

"He seems nice," Tamzyn joked once they hit the footpath, out of earshot.

Michelle glanced back. Fredrick was standing in the centre of a ring of security guards regaling his comrades with the details of the detectives' enquiry.

"A nice gossip," Michelle commented.

"Should we file a report?"

"Looks like our visit will do the trick. Best keep this one off the books," Michelle confirmed.

"Back to headquarters then?"

They arrived at Parliament Train Station.

"Tessa's waiting for me at the library. I'll see you tomorrow."

"No worries." Tamzyn looked uneasy. "What should I tell Chom we were doing?"

Michelle laughed. "Tell the boss we were helping a concerned business owner with her communications."

# 2

Michelle and Cameron watched the sunset from the backyard while they listened to Tessa cook.

"Salacious," Cameron remarked.

Michelle's stories about her workday usually involved stolen property, bad behaviour or the occasional break-in.

"Annie's so polite, nothing seems quite so sordid when she's involved," Michelle said.

"If those walls could talk." Cameron grinned.

"They would never talk." Michelle laughed. Annie's walls would be as discreet as their owner.

Tessa dropped a pot and screamed as it hit the floor. The sound of sticky liquid sloshing projected to their deckchairs.

Michelle went inside to assess the damage.

Tessa was hunched over their dinner strewn across the kitchen.

"Do you need some help?" Michelle asked tenderly.

Tessa had recently proclaimed she needed to learn how to cook all her favourite meals before moving out.

"I have to cook the pasta again," Tessa sulked. She was perpetually angst-ridden.

"I'll get the mop," Michelle offered.

Michelle was certain Tessa's pensiveness was a by-product of having two parents with dangerous jobs. Cameron, an arborist, was never far from a rickety ladder and a chainsaw.

"Thanks, Mum," Tessa sighed, relieved for the assistance.

Michelle pushed the slush into the centre of the tiles and used a dustpan to scoop the mushy strands into a bucket.

Tessa began her second attempt at spaghetti bolognaise.

"No harm done. I'll wait outside with Dad," Michelle encouraged, not wanting to undermine Tessa's independence.

Michelle and Cameron suspected preparing to leave home was Tessa's way of controlling what she could amidst the pressure of her final year of high school.

When Michelle returned to the deck, Cameron was crouched in a flowerbed.

"I leave you alone for two seconds," she teased.

"The weeds were annoying me. Is she alright?" Cameron asked, returning to his chair.

"No burns, just a bit wet. She's wearing Ugg boots."

Reassured, Cameron revived their conversation. "Do you think the scare tactic will work? I would have thought hundreds of people work in the parliament building."

"No idea. Annie has her ways," Michelle said, she loved her job, never a dull day.

"I wonder if the vandal was a jilted lover?" Cameron fancied himself a detective by association.

Annie would never tell, and Michelle knew better than to ask.

"Sorry, you're going to have to die wondering," Michelle said, quashing his speculation.

Cameron laughed. "I'll add it to the list, along with who kidnapped Harold Holt!"

# 3

Tamzyn stepped into Michelle's office with a bacon and egg roll in one hand and a takeaway coffee in the other. "Chom wants to see us."

"About?" Michelle replied, chasing her muesli with tea.

"Don't know." Tamzyn shrugged. "Chom tried calling you but he couldn't get through?"

Michelle checked her phone. There were three missed calls from their boss. "My phone was on silent. Is he in his office?"

Chewing, Tamzyn nodded.

Michelle left the last of her breakfast and they headed to the lift.

"Must be something serious, he's never in this early," Michelle guessed. "How was your evening?"

Michelle and Tamzyn started their shifts at dawn. Chomley didn't care, so long as the crimes got solved.

"Times tables, chaos, then more times tables," Tamzyn shared affectionally. She never complained, Tamzyn loved her raucous brood of boys.

"Time flies," Michelle reminisced, thinking back to when Tessa was that age.

Tamzyn smiled, grateful to have been paired with a partner who understood her home life.

The lift sprung open and Tamzyn yelped as she nearly collided with Chom.

"There you are," Chom grumbled and stomped off in the direction of Michelle's office.

Chomley, once a spirited detective, had been rendered perpetually grumpy by his office-dwelling managerial position.

Chom helped himself to Michelle's desk chair.

"Close the door, Tamzyn. This conversation requires privacy."

Michelle and Tamzyn glanced at the rows of empty desks outside Michelle's window.

Tamzyn sensed Chom wasn't in the mood for a joke and obediently closed the door and shut the blinds.

"Detectives, a very disturbing incident occurred yesterday," Chom stated intensely, folded his arms, then paused and stared at them.

Michelle had worked with Chom for decades. It was unlike him to afford urgency to anything. He'd seen it all. 'Crimes will still be there for solving after morning tea' was his mantra.

They waited in suspense.

"The mace has been stolen," Chom announced, followed by a prolonged exhale.

Tamzyn looked to Michelle who'd assumed an equally puzzled expression.

"Chom, what's the mace?" Michelle asked awkwardly.

"The Ceremonial Mace from Parliament," Chom replied. Their faces remained blank. "It's like a giant wand, full of power."

Chomley's attempt to convey the hefty significance of the instrument was thwarted by his analogy and Tamzyn burst into laughter.

Chom glared furiously.

"Sorry, Chom," Tamzyn said, turning to Michelle for backup.

"So something important has been stolen from Parliament," Michelle intervened. "Why did you call us?"

"Madame Brussels may have been involved. Annie's a closed book. I know you two used to be close. I was hoping she would talk to you."

Tamzyn wore her trademark raised eyebrow.

Chom wasn't aware of their visit to Parliament yesterday.

"Doesn't sound like Annie?" Michelle said nonchalantly. Annie would never condone such overt escalation.

"I was advised Madame Brussels may have been involved. I don't know any more than that. I hope it's a prank and we can get this thing back quickly and quietly."

Chom frowned at his detectives dismissively then registered his location and stood up to leave. "Any questions?"

Michelle had a plethora of questions but was eclipsed by her partner.

"Given the, um, sensitivity, where should we start?" Tamzyn enquired. There was no standard operating procedure for robbery of a magic government wand.

"Security are expecting you at the crime scene. The building isn't open yet. You should be able to get in and out without raising any suspicions on a Saturday."

"Sorry, Chom. If this thing is so big, why all the secrecy? Isn't everyone going to realise it's not there?" Tamzyn said, confused. "How long is it?"

Chom read from his pocket notebook. "About four feet, gold, sparkly and has a crown."

"That doesn't sound like a wand," Tamzyn commented earnestly.

"It's not a wand, it's a mace!" Chom snapped. "Any more questions?"

"All good, we're on it. I'll update you as soon as we get back," Michelle assured him.

"It goes without saying, detectives, but let's get this one solved, shut, and then bury the paperwork."

Chom stomped towards Tamzyn. She leapt out of his path, then Chom flung the door open and left.

Some of their colleagues had arrived during the meeting. Michelle quickly closed the door before Tamzyn unleashed her thoughts.

"He won't leave his office for a double homicide but a magic wand gets him down here!"

"You'd better wipe that smile off your face before we get to Parliament," Michelle scolded.

"Come on, this is hysterical. Do you think Annie knows who did it?"

Michelle grabbed her cereal bowl, phone, and a fresh notepad. Coincidences were hard to come by in their line of work.

"Let's keep Annie out of this. The kit's in the car. Grab the camera and I'll meet you at the lift," Michelle said, ignoring Tamzyn's whimsy.

Tamzyn pouted, disappointed by her partner's professionalism.

"Two days in a row," Michelle ruminated. "What was that doorkeeper's name?"

"Fredrick Davis," Tamzyn answered. "Think whoever stole the mace cut Annie's phone line?"

"I don't think anything yet." Michelle locked her office door. "Fortunately for us, our new friend Fredrick seems to know more than he's letting on."

# 4

A tram rattled past the detective's unmarked police vehicle. Fredrick lifted the boom gate and they drove into the empty staff car park next to Parliament House.

Compared with his cheery smile the day before, Fredrick appeared forlorn.

"Morning, Fredrick," Tamzyn called brightly as she stepped out the car. "I hear you've lost your mace."

"Something like that, Detective. I apologise, I don't remember your names," Fredrick said, frazzled.

"I'm Detective Nixon and this is Senior Detective Ward."

Fredrick let them in through the side door. The air inside was stale. "I don't know what you've been told. Do you want to see the case?"

"Assume we know nothing, Fredrick. Start from the beginning, please," Michelle advised kindly.

Fredrick paused pensively at the entrance to the Legislative Assembly Chamber then led them past the dispatch boxes to the centre of the hall.

"Detectives, the mace sits on this stand when Parliament is sitting. Otherwise it's kept in its case in the Speaker's Chamber.

I'll take you there now," Fredrick said as if he was conducting a tour, then proceeded to his next stop.

Michelle had been to the parliament building many times before but, cold and vacant, it felt like they'd been transported back in time.

The trio entered a private hallway. When they reached the Speaker's Chamber, Fredrick unlocked the door and turned on the light.

"Historically the Speaker used to live in this room but now it's just an office," Fredrick said and moved out of their way to allow the detectives to see for themselves. "The case is the original. It has two locks. You can see where they've been pried open."

Michelle could see grubby fingerprints on the case and the adjacent windowsill. Tamzyn consulted their kit and prepared to collect the evidence.

"Fredrick, who discovered the case was empty?" Michelle asked while she took photos of the disfigured clasps.

"I did. Yesterday, just after lunch. I was leaving a package on the desk and light from the window reflected off the broken locks which caught my eye. The case was ajar so I peeked through the crack and saw that the mace was gone. I notified George immediately. I didn't touch a thing."

"Who's George?" Tamzyn asked while she applied dust to the oily ridges. Fredrick clearly thought the detectives had more information than they did.

"George Pearse is the housekeeper," Fredrick clarified, mesmerised by their seamless teamwork.

"I imagine lots of people would have access to this room. Any clue why someone would steal the mace?" Michelle questioned.

"No, it's not worth anything. The mace is just coated with gold, underneath its cheap metal. Everyone who works here knows that," he replied defensively.

"Fredrick, I noticed there are security cameras throughout the building. Have you reviewed yesterday's footage?" Michelle pressed.

"There are no cameras in this office because the Speaker deals with confidential matters. We checked the tape from the hallway, no one entered the room. They must have used the window."

Tamzyn finished the fingerprinting.

"Do you have any recent photos of the mace?" Michelle asked as Tamzyn packed up their equipment.

"We have some postcards in the gift shop. I'll be back in a minute." Fredrick dashed out the open door.

"So the mace isn't valuable," Tamzyn commented.

"If we don't get any hits off the fingerprints or the security video, this is going to be tricky."

"You mean impossible. Anyone could have taken it. Why does Chom think Annie's involved?"

"No idea. Let's get out of here," Michelle said, mindful of their orders.

Fredrick returned and handed a selection of photos to Tamzyn who placed them in the kit.

"Thanks, Fredrick. Before we head off, one last question. You mentioned the mace is kept in this case until its needed for Parliament. When will people notice its missing?"

"The next sitting week starts on Tuesday."

"What happens if the mace isn't back by then?" Tamzyn added.

"I don't know," Fredrick admitted.

Fredrick took them back to the carpark. Tamzyn handed him her card.

"I'll have the security tapes to you by the end of the day," Fredrick promised then left for the gatehouse to let them out.

Tamzyn waved goodbye as they pulled out towards Collins Street. "The timing doesn't make sense. Fredrick claims he discovered the mace was missing at lunchtime on Friday and immediately told the housekeeper. Then what? They didn't call the police until late last night."

"Mmmm," Michelle pondered. She was concentrating on navigating the traffic, the city roads were busy for a weekend.

"Cover up?" Tamzyn suggested.

"But if it's not valuable, then why call us at all?"

"And what about Annie?"

Michelle's measly breakfast was wearing off and she was too hungry to think. She didn't want to involve Annie if it could be avoided but there was almost nothing else to go on. She could feel it in the pit of her empty stomach, they were missing something.

# 5

Michelle knocked then opened the office door and poked her head in. "Are you free?"

"What do you need?" Chom barked busily. He did paperwork on Saturdays.

"Mace mystery. Do you have time to talk strategy?"

Chom was face down in a file. It was unusual to see hard copy, paper was reserved for highly sensitive matters.

"Yes," Chom replied without looking up.

Michelle seated herself under the window overlooking the Yarra River and waited for her boss to realise she required his full attention.

Fredrick had delivered the security footage. It had taken Tamzyn all of five minutes to confirm Fredrick's account. The mace had been replaced by the Serjeant-at-Arms after Parliament finished sitting on Thursday just before 1am Friday morning. Fredrick had discovered the mace was missing a touch before 1pm on Friday then returned five minutes later with George Pearse. In the intervening twelve hours, Susan Hadly, the charwoman, had cleaned the office at 7am.

"What aren't you telling me?" Michelle interrupted Chom's reading.

"I told you everything this morning," Chom refuted. He knew he'd given them a nightmare to wrangle.

"You didn't tell me anything this morning. Who called you? Why do you think Annie's involved? Why did it take them half a day to report the crime? Should I go on?"

Chom grimaced guiltily and consulted his faithful notepad. "The Serjeant-at-Arms called me personally last night. He'd been instructed by the Speaker to call the police quietly after the Speaker had spent the afternoon calling staff to find out where the mace had been taken and finally concluded it had been stolen."

"And Annie?"

"The Serjeant-at-Arms had heard from a clerk called… William Robinson apparently, that we were investigating the phone lines being cut at Madam Brussels and assumed the two incidents were connected." Chom eyed Michelle suspiciously. "Given we have no such investigation, I assumed that was you."

Michelle blushed. "I was just doing Annie a favour. Regardless, she would never engage in retaliation."

Michelle was disappointed, their only lead wasn't a lead at all.

"Nonetheless I doubt there's anything sinister behind the timing. So if I take your word that Annie isn't involved, and the staff didn't see anything, where does that leave us?" Chom asked while rummaging around his snack draw.

Michelle watched the fading sunlight flicker across the skyscrapers lining the river while she thought. No suspects, no motive, no witnesses, no evidence.

"No match for the fingerprints, no ransom demand and nothing on the security tapes leaves us at square one," she replied.

Chom munched on an apricot square and shuffled over to the

couch to share his treat with Michelle.

"If the mace isn't found by Tuesday when Parliament resumes, people will find out it was stolen. So we should go public now and ask if anyone saw anything. Someone trundling around the city with a mace would be fairly memorable."

"You think an inside job?" Chom asked.

"Doubtful. According to the doorman it's common knowledge that the mace isn't worth anything," Michelle advised. An apricot sugar rush hit her temples.

"I'll try and convince the Serjeant-at-Arms that a public appeal is the best shot we've got. Other than embarrassing, the theft appears to be inconsequential," Chom agreed and returned to his desk.

"That remains to be seen. Who knows where we'll find it," Michelle joked. She missed working with her former partner.

Chom grinned. "Touché."

Chom had grown into his leadership role and emulated the seriousness it required. Every now and then, however, the cheeky officer Chom had been fleetingly reappeared.

Michelle got up to leave. Cameron and Tessa were meeting her in Flinders Lane for dinner.

"I'll wait to hear from you on the appeal. Anything else?" Michelle asked.

"Keep an open mind. I know you think Annie's not involved but that doesn't mean one of her girls doesn't know something," Chom cautioned.

Michelle knew she had a blind spot when it came to people she cared about. "Yes, Boss."

# 6

Chom had assembled the usual gaggle of crime reporters and pleaded with their Sunday night audiences to come forward if they'd seen the mace.

On Monday morning Tamzyn had been inundated with calls from nosy speculators. By the afternoon, however, Chom's appeal had produced two genuine leads.

The first, Reverend Dr Llewyn Bevan, had been asked by a parishioner to deliver a message to the police but the reverend would only discuss the matter in person.

The second, a tram driver named James Merrick, had noticed a passenger carrying a mace-shaped package which matched Chom's description on the news.

Tamzyn had lodged a request for the security footage from the tram while Michelle arranged a meeting at the reverend's church.

The reverend stood at the top of the steps farewelling his departing flock. The detectives waited in their vehicle as the congregation egressed.

"He looks happy for someone with information about a serious crime," Tamzyn commented flippantly. She unbuckled her seatbelt, drained the last of her coffee and plucked gum from the dashboard.

"Don't be blasphemous, and don't call the mace a wand in front of the reverend," Michelle cautioned.

Tamzyn's humour tended to unnerve civilians.

The reverend ended his conversation when he noticed Michelle and Tamzyn hovering by their car, and waved.

"You must be the detectives. Who was I speaking with on the phone?"

"That was me. I'm Detective Tamzyn Nixon and this is Senior Detective Michelle Ward. Please, call me Tamzyn."

"Welcome. Thank you for coming. People expect me to be here for them, I hope you understand."

They followed the reverend through a glorious archway.

"No problem at all. We appreciate any help we can get."

The hall was small and inviting with beautiful carvings and stained glass.

"Your church is stunning, Reverend," Tamzyn commented.

"Thank you, Tamzyn. It's a joy to spend my days here," the Reverend agreed.

Inside the church the pews were empty. The reverend led them through the centre aisle and out into an antechamber to the side of a towering organ. They arrived at his office and gathered around a small round table next to a courtyard overflowing with vines and ornaments.

"I must admit, Reverend, I was surprised to receive your call. I was under the impression you're bound by some form of confidentiality?" Michelle said, pulling out her notepad.

"I respect the privacy of my parishioners. However in this matter, I am, shall we say, an envoy."

"I see. Thank you for clarifying." Michelle began scribbling.

"Forgive me, Detectives, this message is rather awkward." The reverend blushed.

Tamzyn's eyebrow shot up. Michelle imparted a corrective frown and Tamzyn replaced her smirk with a serious expression.

"I have been advised by a parishioner that they saw the mace in the lobby of a brothel near Parliament. They are a customer of the establishment and do not wish to be identified."

"Reverend, do you know the name of the brothel?" Tamzyn probed.

"Sorry, Detectives. He disclosed only that he saw the mace leaning against an armchair in the lobby. Apparently it was quite obviously out of place." The reverend's cheeks burned.

Tamzyn noted the parishioner's conflicting sense of morality.

"Did your parishioner mention the time?" Michelle asked.

"He said it wasn't in the lobby when he arrived. He saw it when he left at around 2am. I'm afraid that's all I was told."

"This is all very useful. Please pass on our thanks," Tamzyn said, excited their appeal had gleaned a real sighting. She had started to become disillusioned.

The reverend consulted his modern computer, out-of-place on an opulent desk. "I'm glad I could help. Detectives, I have some matters to attend to before my next meeting. Would you be able to find your way out?"

"Of course, Reverend," Michelle said finishing her note.

"I hope this information proves fruitful and will pass on your thanks." The reverend hurriedly closed the office door behind them.

Tamzyn restrained her thoughts until they were safely encased by the police car. "Well, I know where I've seen an armchair in the lobby of a brothel recently."

Heeding Chomley's advice to keep an open mind, Michelle reluctantly agreed. "It certainly sounds like Madame Brussels."

# 7

Tessa studied her mother's technique while Michelle prepared stuffing for the roast chicken. She scrawled furiously in her recipe notebook as Michelle dictated the steps.

Michelle relished afternoons with Tessa. Her daughter forgot to put up her guard when they cooked together, which allowed Michelle to feel like a good parent for a few moments each day.

"How many people does this feed?" Tessa asked as though she hadn't eaten the dish weekly since she was old enough to digest solids.

"There are three of us, then soup with the leftovers," Michelle replied, warmed by Tessa's resolve. "How was school?"

"I got an A in my Calculus test."

Michelle heard a quiver, Tessa sounded preoccupied. "That's great. How's Amanda?"

Amanda had been 'going through something' according to Tessa who became discombobulated whenever her best friend wavered from perfection.

"She's good. It's just been a weird week. Our science teacher quit, and no one knows why. And there's all this drama with the teachers and they're really distracted and emotional," Tessa explained, sketching the raw chicken.

"I'm sorry to hear that. I'm sure it will blow over," Michelle encouraged positively, disguising her concern.

"Can I do the carrots?" Tessa perked up now her worries had been offloaded.

Michelle smiled and slid the bag and peeler across the counter.

"How was your day, Mum?"

"The mace mystery got a whole lot more mysterious," Michelle joked.

Like her father, Tessa loved helping solve Michelle's cases. They'd spent many memorable nights on the back deck devising elaborate theories. However, the crimes assigned to Michelle and Tamzyn were usually G-rated.

"Chom said on the news that the mace isn't worth anything. So why would anyone take it?" Tessa asked.

Michelle dreaded to think what it may have been doing in Annie's lobby.

"We don't know yet, we're still chasing down leads." Michelle's hand was inside the chicken when her phone buzzed. "Can you check that for me, please."

Tessa wiped carrot juice off her hands and unlocked Michelle's phone. It was a message from Tamzyn.

"It's a photo of a wrench," Tessa conveyed, confused. She held up the phone so Michelle could see the image. "I don't get it."

"Neither do I." Michelle laughed. "Can you please call her."

Tessa rolled her eyes and dialled.

"Hi, it's Tessa. Mum's cooking chicken." Tessa nodded as Tamzyn spoke. "Yeah, I'm free Saturday night. I'll check with Dad to see if he can drive me and let you know."

Tessa appeared to have forgotten why she had called Tamzyn. Michelle mouthed 'wrench'.

"Mum wants to know why you sent her a wrench?" Tessa said then listened to the reply. "Ohhh, Mum, it's not a wrench. It's a spanner. A spanner in the works."

Michelle laughed. Typical Tamzyn, her humour made their menial tasks tenable.

"Can you put her on speaker?"

Tessa set the phone down on top of a canister and returned to the carrots.

"I thought you understood me," Tamzyn teased.

"You're an enigma. What have you got?" Michelle replied then added, "Tessa can hear you."

"So, I reviewed the video from the tram, and I found the guy James was talking about. It looks like the mace in the package, thus the spanner."

"Could you see where the guy got on and off the tram?" Michelle asked while she coated the chicken with spices.

Tessa notated diligently.

"The suspect got on alone with the package about a block from Parliament near the Exhibition Building, didn't talk to anyone, then got off about ten minutes later at Johnson Street."

"Do you need to go?" Michelle could hear Tamzyn's children screeching in the background.

"They're fine." Tamzyn laughed. "I think we need to go back to Parliament and ask the staff if anyone knows this guy. If it isn't an inside job, how would he know where to find the case?"

"I agree. Also, I want to talk to the charwoman to see whether she noticed the locks were broken when she was cleaning."

"Sounds like a plan. I think an impromptu visit is better."

Michelle weighed the pros and cons. "Alright, see you in the morning."

"Tessa, babysitting, message me," Tamzyn shouted then hung up.

Tessa admired her newly recorded recipe, one meal closer to adulthood.

Michelle heard Cameron pull into the driveway, the sign it was time for Michelle to triple check her daughter was thoroughly vented of her day while Cameron cleaned his work tools.

"I'll call the school tomorrow and make sure they've got their act together before exams," Michelle reassured Tessa, placing the pan in the oven.

"Thanks, Mum," Tessa said, hugging Michelle then retreated to her bedroom to begin her homework.

Savouring another cherished conversation with her daughter, Michelle watched Tessa walk away. She was all too aware, soon, she would be preparing dinner on her own.

# 8

Chom and Tamzyn sat opposite James Merrik. Sweat had formed a row of beads above James' eyebrows.

Tamzyn hadn't been expecting the witness to react so anxiously to sitting in an interview room.

"James, thank you for volunteering to talk to us. This is the breakthrough we were hoping for," Chom lauded, trying to calm the tram driver's misplaced nerves.

"Thank you, Sir. Just doing my duty," James replied, beginning to hyperventilate.

"You mentioned on the phone, James, that the man you saw carrying the package is one of your regulars. Can you please tell us a bit more about what happened that day?" Tamzyn asked.

James relaxed momentarily while he focused on recalling the memory.

"I remembered it because he normally gets on in the morning at Johnston Street and gets the tram the other way in the evening. Has done for years, which is why I noticed him in the middle of the day. Also, the package clanged loudly against one of the hand-rails when he got off the tram. That's what made me think it might have been that pole you're looking for," James blurted speedily as though he might forget what he'd seen if he slowed down.

"Do you think you would recognise your passenger if you saw him on the street, or in a café, or in a line up?" Chom queried.

In his experience, witnesses had a hard time recognising people they saw all the time in different settings.

"Absolutely, no doubt."

"That's great. Thanks, James. A couple more questions and we'll be done here," Tamzyn said. "When the man boarded the tram with the package, did he get on at the same place he usually gets on in the evening?"

"A couple of stops away. He normally gets on outside Parliament. That day, he was up near the Royal Exhibition Building," James replied, confirming his earlier story and the video evidence.

"And do you know where he works? Have you ever noticed a uniform or badges, name tags, hats, anything like that?" Tamzyn prompted.

"No. It's always hectic during peak hour and I'm concentrating on driving, but also I don't always drive that line."

"Thank you, James. Is there anything else you think we should know before we wrap up?"

"Nothing I can think off, Detective. He looks so normal. You just never know these days," James remarked, relaxing now the formalities had concluded.

"Books and covers, James." Chom slapped him on the back like an old friend. "Tamzyn will see you out. Thanks again for your service."

"Thank you, Sir." James blushed.

Tamzyn led James out of the interview room and Chom grinned at Michelle through the mirror before he joined her in the adjoining recording studio.

Chom opened the door to find Michelle chuckling to herself.

"You're quite the performer," Michelle said. She had been watching the exchange.

"He was suspiciously nervous. Should we start an investigation into him?" Chom joked.

Most suspects reacted the same way to that room, whether they were guilty or not.

"Two equally credible sightings, two completely different stories," Michelle posed, cutting straight to the crux.

While the tip line had yielded potentially contradictory accounts, Michelle was nonetheless relieved they were inching closer toward a suspect, though still no motive.

"What are we thinking? The mace is taken to Annie's in the middle of the night, then returned, then stolen separately the next morning," Chom theorised sceptically.

"Highly unlikely," Michelle countered, brow furrowed.

Tamzyn returned. "He's a sweetheart. What did I miss?"

"We were just debating whether the mace sighting at Annie's might have been on a different night before it was stolen," Michelle replied.

"Interesting." Tamzyn considered the possibility. "We didn't make the announcement until Sunday. It also could have been at Madame Brussels after it had been stolen on Friday or Saturday night."

They all nodded.

"Tamzyn, can you please invite Fredrick to come in to view the tram's security footage? He'll know if the guy works in the building," Michelle asked.

Chom grunted in agreement.

"Sure thing." Tamzyn called Fredrick's number.

"I still need to talk to the charwoman to try and figure out the time of the theft. You would think that if she cleans the case every day, she would have noticed that the locks were broken," Michelle said to Chom over Tamzyn's conversation with Fredrick.

"This is just getting stranger and stranger," Chom replied.

Tamzyn hung up the phone. "Fredrick will be here in an hour."

# 9

Michelle was tired. She'd had a restless night trying to reconcile why someone would go to such lengths to acquire an object that was inherently worthless. After hours of eluding sleep, Michelle decided, in order to tether the thief and the theft, she needed to learn more about the mace.

George Pearse had been called away on an urgent errand and had left Michelle to peruse the museum in the basement of the Old Treasury Building while she waited.

Michelle read the educational placards which explained the building's past importance to its present-day admirers. There was nothing in the exhibition about the origins of the mace.

Michelle ran her fingers over the cold stone. Like the empty Parliament at dawn, the preserved gold bank vault transported her into antiquity.

George returned to continue their meeting smelling strongly of paint thinner.

"A pen mark on the wall outside the surviving Premiers' offices needed to be removed. There are different standards for what constitutes an emergency with these people." George rolled his eyes. "Shall we go for a walk?"

"That would be lovely," Michelle replied. She didn't get as much exercise as she'd like.

George led Michelle back up to the ground floor and they ambled toward Fitzroy Gardens.

The sunshine on her skin was energising. The police headquarters building was oppressively concrete, it was refreshing to be surrounded by nature.

"I appreciate you making the time to meet me. Fredrick suggested you would be able to answer some technical questions about the mace," Michelle explained. George was clearly a pivotal member of the staff.

"I'm happy to help. The robbery is being portrayed as a bit of a joke by the media, but it's really quite a vicious attack."

"Really, why is that?"

"I suspect most Victorians would not be privy to the formalities of the Chamber. The mace represents the constitutional rights of the people. It's symbolic of the authority which is vested in the Speaker of the House to conduct Parliament. For example, when the mace is not in the Chamber, Parliament cannot proceed, even if the Speaker is there. The power of the people resides in the mace."

"I was under the impression the mace was just ceremonial?"

"It is ceremonial. But ceremony matters here. If someone was going to steal something from the building to signify a threat to Parliament, it would be hard to find an object more potently symbolic than the mace."

Michelle blushed. She was taken aback by George's eloquence. Chom wasn't too far off when he'd described the mace as a powerful wand. The detectives had assumed the motive was benign or, at worst, financial. Michelle pondered whether the mace's worth was not measured in currency.

They passed a pond covered with lily pads. A duck glided effortlessly across the surface followed by a brood of ducklings.

"Fredrick told us that the mace is worthless and that all the staff knew that," Michelle remarked, keen to hear George's perspective.

"The mace is silver with a gold coating. It has a garland with roses and eucalypts, and a crown which represents England, Ireland, Scotland and Victoria. It's the intricate craftsmanship which makes the mace look valuable. We all know the composition because we maintain it. The mace is hollow so it can be dismantled and transported if Parliament is sitting elsewhere in the state. We take it apart to clean it."

Listening to the gravitas with which George spoke, Michelle realised its materials were irrelevant to the majesty the mace was intended to evoke. Significance she felt for the first time.

Michelle took a moment to digest the information. It was curious that the mace was compactable. Perhaps the man on the tram hadn't the skill or the time to conceal their crime.

"George, the mace was stolen from its case in the Speaker's Chamber. How would anyone other than the staff know where the mace is stored?"

Michelle tried to sound inquisitorial not accusatorial. Fortunately George was partial to abstractions.

"The location of the case isn't confidential, it's mentioned in our tours when we discuss the role of the mace when we take visitors into the Legislative Assembly. Also, the architectural layout would be easy to obtain through many different public sources. Visitors are always fascinated with the construction of this building."

They reached a fork in the path and swung back toward the building.

Tamzyn and Michelle had assumed that the window had been used to access the Speaker's Chamber to avoid the security camera. However, if the thief didn't have access to the building, the window may have just been the easiest option.

"Interesting. Fredrick told me you know the mace better than anyone. Do you have any theories as to why someone would steal it?"

George thought about her question.

"I don't," he concluded. "But I can honestly say I don't believe anyone employed here was involved. I have worked here for decades. I can't think of anyone who would even fathom such a betrayal."

"Thank you, George. You have given me a lot to think about. I appreciate you sharing your knowledge."

"You're most welcome."

His conviction was convincing but, nonetheless, money and greed were powerful motivators.

George admired the Old Treasury as they approached the start of the trail. "I am enamoured with these buildings."

Michelle smiled. She was impressed that George's affection for Parliament hadn't been stifled by the grubbiness of politics.

Her phone vibrated. She checked the message and found another spanner from Tamzyn.

"It was a pleasure meeting you, George. I hope we can find the mace for you."

"So do I, Michelle."

Michelle and Tamzyn had been wondering why the Serjeant-at-Arms didn't just commission a new mace. It was clear to Michelle now. To those who truly understood its meaning, the mace was irreplaceable.

# 10

Tamzyn was with Fredrick, so Michelle left her a note and went upstairs to see Chomley.

Chom's door was open. He was face down in a box of noodles with one eye on the computer screen.

"Mace mystery update?" he asked.

"Of sorts. Should I wait?" Michelle snapped, irritated by his split focus.

Chom turned off the screen and mockingly put his noodles to one side. "Proceed."

"Thank you." Decades of friendship had earned Michelle the privilege of being snarky without requiring a reason. "I've just been speaking to the housekeeper, George. I was worried we didn't fully understand the significance of the mace."

"And?"

"We haven't talked about the possibility of political interference."

Chom scoffed. "Why would we? No one knows what the bloody thing is, including you."

Michelle ignored his retort. "Did you know that Parliament can't sit unless the mace is in the room. I wonder if someone was trying to stop Parliament sitting?"

"Yes, I did, and I told you that the Speaker checked the old mace out of the museum so there was no disruption."

"But someone trying to delay Parliament probably wouldn't have known the Speaker could just use an old mace. We didn't even know they had an old mace," Michelle argued.

"What are you thinking?" Chom said, reaching for the carton.

Michelle gave him a disapproving glare and he withdrew his hand.

"After I spoke with George, I went and had a chat with the charwoman, Susan Hadley. She hadn't noticed anything unusual when she cleaned the Speaker's Chamber the morning the mace was taken. But while I was there I picked up this list of bills being debated this week." Michelle handed him the schedule. "What if someone was trying to stop one of these bills becoming law?"

"It's a good theory," Chom admitted, annoyed he hadn't thought of it himself. The detective in Chomley hated second place. "What about Annie and the tram guy, how do they factor?"

"I'm not sure yet. Tamzyn's on tram guy now and I haven't seen Annie yet, but my gut says she's not involved."

Chom's gut was certain Annie was involved, but Tamzyn burst into his office before he could offer his contrary instinct.

Tamzyn hurried over and slid into the empty chair next to Michelle.

"We were just talking motives," Michelle said. "How'd things go with Fredrick?"

Tamzyn lit up. Chom seized the opportunity to sneak a mouthful of noodles.

"Very, very well. Fredrick identified tram man as their engineer, Thomas Jeffrey. Fredrick was absolutely shocked. Apparently

Thomas' father worked as the engineer before Thomas and Thomas has been working at the parliament building his whole life. Even with the evidence in front of him, Fredrick didn't believe that Thomas was involved. I kept him talking, hoping he was just in shock and would arrive at some form of acceptance, but he just kept repeating that there must have been something else in the package. He was very compelling. I almost believe him."

Chom grunted with relief. "Finally a suspect."

Michelle was surprised. George had been adamant none of his staff were involved. She had thought they wouldn't be able to identify the man in the video.

"How did you leave things with Fredrick?" Michelle asked, worried Fredrick would forewarn Thomas Jeffrey before they had a chance to get a warrant.

"All over it. I had him sign a Statutory Declaration. There was no way he was going to keep his mouth shut." Tamzyn grinned.

Chom picked up the phone to call the magistrate. "I'll get the search warrant. Let's try and get there tonight."

Michelle and Tamzyn pulled out their phones as they made their way back to their floor to notify their husbands it would be a late night.

They ordered takeaway for dinner. As they waited for the warrant to be issued, Michelle filled Tamzyn in on her discussions with George Pearse and Susan Hadley, and their new theory that someone was trying to derail Parliament.

Tamzyn inspected the list of bills. There were twelve. It would take some time to compile a list of potentially aggrieved parties.

"I didn't realise the mace was so, powerful." Tamzyn laughed, realising the hype probably should have tipped her off. "When we started I thought for sure we had no chance. Now we have four completely different leads."

"Four?" Michelle frowned. "The mace at a brothel from the reverend, Thomas Jeffrey on the tram with the mace from James Merrick and someone trying to stop a bill being passed this week. That's three. What's the fourth?"

"Whoever keeps cutting the phone line at Madame Brussels. Could be the same person trying a different method to get attention. It was Annie who told us she thought it was the jokers at Parliament," Tamzyn reminded her.

"Good point," Michelle agreed. "Four leads it is."

Chomley appeared in the doorway. "We've got the warrant."

# 11

Michelle walked up Annie's cobbled driveway. Unlike Annie, her mansion was theatrical and overt.

Michelle rang the bell.

Annie lived alone. It was impossible to tell from the outside whether she was at home.

The door inched open with the chain still attached.

"No phone call?" Annie asked through the sliver.

Michelle could see a glass of wine in her hand and a book under her arm.

"No time. Do you have a minute?"

Annie unclasped the guard, allowing Michelle into her toasty, aroma filled foyer.

"Would you like some chardonnay?"

"Thanks, but not tonight. We have a big day tomorrow."

After the warrant had been issued, Tamzyn had discovered Thomas Jeffrey's wife, Elizabeth, was gravely ill with leukemia and they had several young children. As a result, Chomley had decided to delay the search of their family home until school hours.

Annie led Michelle through to the kitchen where she was brewing sauces and jams.

"Are you hungry?" Annie asked as she put down the book and concurrently turned a blackberry jam and folded a bitter smelling chutney. The fragrances were oddly complementary.

"We ate at work, but thanks," Michelle replied.

Annie wasn't interested in small talk and waited for Michelle to reveal the reason for the intrusion.

"Thanks for seeing me at home. We're mid-breakthrough in a case and it's time sensitive."

Annie nodded understandingly.

"Have you seen the news reports that the mace was stolen from Parliament last week?" Michelle asked.

"I have."

"We're following several leads." Michelle pulled out a snapshot of Thomas Jeffrey from the tram. "Do you recognise this man?"

Annie put down her utensils and inspected the photo. "Not in the slightest. Who is he?"

She handed back the photo and tasted the chutney. Unimpressed, she added brown sugar.

"He may have been seen with the mace." Michelle paused to consider how to frame her next question. "We also received an anonymous tip that the mace may have been in your lobby."

Michelle braced for Annie's reaction.

"Shouldn't you be questioning me in an interrogation room?"

"You're not a suspect. I'm just following up on the tip in order to rule it out."

Annie turned off the stove and placed her hands on the counter.

"Do you not think I would have called you if I had information relevant to your case?" Annie said smiling.

"I do think you would call me and I also know nothing gets by you which is why I'm here to ask you myself. The tip is credible," Michelle replied, Annie's apparent amusement was inexplicable.

"Your snitch didn't see the mace in our lobby." Annie reached for her wine and allowed the suspense to build. Michelle's exacerbation was palpable. "We have a mace."

"What!" Michelle blurted.

"We have our own mace."

"What do you mean?"

"I can't be any clearer, Michelle. We have a mace. We have a scale replica of the mace." Annie laughed.

"I'm sorry. I don't understand. Why!"

"It is, shall we say, a longing of one of our clients to be the Speaker of the House."

"That's absurd!"

Stunned, nervous laughter overtook her and Michelle melted onto the bench.

"I don't judge. I am merely a conduit. If you ask me at the precinct I will lie and if you ask for the tape from the lobby I will wipe it."

Annie poured sparking apple juice into a glass for Michelle.

"So what should I write in my report. That I asked you and you said it wasn't there?"

Annie feigned consideration and smiled sweetly. "Yes, that would suit me well."

Michelle wasn't going to lie, Annie knew that. Michelle moved them forward.

"Sorry I can't stay long. I just have one more question."

Annie shot Michelle an impatient look, she was bored with the conversation.

"Tamzyn thinks the person who cut your phone line might have stolen the mace. Did you figure out who it was? It would be helpful if we could rule out a connection," Michelle asked cautiously. She didn't want to worry Annie unnecessarily.

Annie stiffened. "No, we didn't. Do you think it's linked?"

"We're still investigating but we haven't ruled anything out yet," Michelle admitted, preparing to leave.

"I'll let you know if it happens again. Will you and Cameron come to dinner next week?" Annie asked as she led Michelle back to the entrance.

Annie was a generous host. Her dinner parties were legendary. Annie's friends spanned all circles and creeds. Consequently each occasion was a unique combination of intriguing and weathered souls.

"I'll let you know if I can get away. This case is all consuming." Michelle embraced her friend.

"I can imagine. People are enthralled. All anyone can talk about is who stole the mace."

Annie smiled knowingly. Her guests were often not very far from the truth.

# 12

Thomas Jeffrey drummed his fingers against the interview table. Tamzyn and Chom watched him from the recording studio, waiting until his anger subsided.

Oddly, Thomas appeared neither nervous nor surprised to be sitting in a Police Station.

They entered and Chom handed him a glass of water.

Thomas grunted and accepted the refreshment.

"Do you know why you're here, Thomas," Tamzyn asked matter-of-factly.

Thomas had been furious when Chomley and Tamzyn had collected him for questioning shortly after he'd stepped off the tram on his way into work.

He slammed his fist on the table. "The mace was stolen and now you're wasting everyone's time constantly turning up and harassing everyone, and we're all sick of it!"

"We're just doing our jobs, Mr Jeffrey. There's no need to yell," Chom said sternly and Thomas unwound slightly.

Chom had not expected the husband of a terminally ill woman to be well reasoned or calm.

Tamzyn slid several photos of Thomas on the tram holding the mace-shaped package across the cold steel. Thomas stared at the images of himself for several seconds then looked up to meet their inquisition.

"That's me on the tram. So what?"

"The package you're holding is the exact size and shape of the mace and you boarded the tram roughly the same time it was taken from your workplace," Tamzyn explained, trying to convey the seriousness of his predicament.

"And?" Thomas yelled at Chom like he couldn't believe what he was hearing.

"Mr Jeffrey, this appears to be you with the mace. Are you claiming this is not the mace?" Chom asked.

Thomas squinted at the package again, closely.

"I don't remember." His face morphed from fury to worry.

"Thomas, this photo was taken a week ago. You can't remember a huge package from last week?" Tamzyn asked pityingly.

"No, my wife is dying. I can't remember what I ate for breakfast, I can't remember how many kids I have," Thomas seethed.

Tamzyn stared into Thomas' sad, pleading eyes and wanted to be believe him.

"You were getting the tram home in the middle of the day. Does that help jog your memory?" Tamzyn prompted.

"No. I get the tram home for lunch often to spend time with Elizabeth when she's having a bad day."

"And do you take large packages home often?" Tamzyn continued, hoping to deconstruct the event.

"All the time. My tools are at home. If there's something that needs mending or altering, I often do it in my shed," Thomas said despondently.

He was melting down and Chom interjected. "Mr Jeffrey, do you mind if I have a chat with Tamzyn outside?"

Thomas nodded, defeated.

They walked around to the recording studio and watched him wait.

"He's not denying it but he's not admitting it either. Do you think Thomas took the mace back to his house for maintenance and forgot?" Tamzyn speculated, trying to find a reason to excuse this miserable man.

"Couldn't be," Chom replied, equally perplexed. "No one went into the Speaker's Chamber."

"Ahh, you're right," Tamzyn realised. "We have to let him go. We can't prove it's the mace in the package."

"You can see the shape of the crown," Chom refuted.

"It could be a table leg or a lamp, we just don't know. We have nothing else," Tamzyn countered.

Through the glass, Thomas Jeffrey was the silhouette of a broken man. Not a scintilla of guilt etched on his face. Just pain.

"He's got no criminal record, no motive, and he's worked at the Parliament his whole life. We might have the most damning photo ever taken, but we've got nothing," Tamzyn argued fervently in favour of their suspect.

"Easy, Counsel," Chom joked.

"Sorry." Tamzyn expected her boss to accuse her of partialism but he didn't. Chom felt just as bad for Thomas.

"Let him go. You're right, and we know where he'll be," Chom agreed mercifully.

When they re-entered the interview room, Thomas Jeffrey raised his head, tears threatening to spill.

"Mr Jeffrey, you're free to leave," Chom informed him and handed Thomas Tamzyn's business card and a copy of the photos of him on the tram. "Should your memory return please inform Tamzyn on this number what was in your package in that photo."

A coarse sigh escaped. Thomas Jeffrey deflated to half his size and placed his forehead on his palms then burst into tears.

"I was sure you were going to arrest me. Thank you, Detectives. Thank you."

"No need to thank us, Mr Jeffrey. Tamzyn will see you out." Chom drew the line at unruly emotions and left the room.

Tamzyn pulled her chair around and sat next to Thomas, tempted to reach out and comfort him.

"I'm so sorry your wife is ill," Tamzyn said, contemplating parenting alone filled her with dread.

"It's horrific." Thomas turned to Tamzyn like he had been waiting for someone to ask him how he really was. "She's just so sick. She's in agony and she's exhausted and I can't help her, and the kids are scared, and I feel... useless."

Thomas' feelings poured out and he began sobbing. There was nothing Tamzyn could say to ease his suffering, so she sat with him while him cried.

# 13

"Who are you?" asked the woman.

Michelle stood pressed against the front brick wall of Thomas Jeffrey's house, trying to avoid the weather.

"My name is Senior Detective Ward. Are you Elizabeth Lennox?"

A patrol car monitored Michelle's approach from the driveway.

"No. I'm Mary Hider. I'm Mrs Lennox's nurse. She's resting." A burley woman appeared. "This is Emily Miller, she takes care of the house."

Emily smiled at Michelle over Mary's shoulder.

They seemed wholesome. Michelle hoped her presence wouldn't frighten them.

"Mr Jeffrey is suspected of being in possession of an item which doesn't belong to him. I'm here to see whether the item is hidden in the house. Mr Jeffrey is waiting at the Police Station."

"Oh my goodness." Mary gasped and consulted Emily. "Shall I check with Mrs Lennox?"

"I'm sorry, Mary. I was unclear. I don't need Mrs Lennox's permission. I have a warrant issued by a magistrate which allows me to search the house."

Michelle handed the warrant to Mary and pointed at the police car.

Mary passed the paper to Emily and gawked at Michelle while Emily scanned the document.

The rain was smashing down on the pavement behind Michelle and water was splashing up the back of her trousers.

"It says here you're looking for a mace," Emily said.

"Yes, you may have seen it on the news." Michelle plucked a photo of the mace from her clipboard and handed it to Mary. "This is what the mace looks like. Have you seen any packages that shape stored in the house?"

They both shook their heads. Mary handed back the photo and continued to block the doorway.

"Thank you for your cooperation. I will have to come in now and have a look around myself," Michelle insisted authoritatively.

Emily tugged at Mary. She had decided it wasn't worth an argument and let Michelle inside.

"I will need to look in every room. Can you please let Mrs Lennox know I'm here. Please assure her there is no cause for alarm. We haven't laid any charges against her husband." Michelle stopped short of adding, *at this stage*.

Emily disappeared upstairs to deliver Michelle's message.

Michelle walked through the downstairs rooms, checking all the cupboards and drawers large enough to conceal the mace in its compact form.

Mary stayed untrustingly glued to Michelle.

"Mary, how long have you worked here?" Michelle asked, lying on the floor feeling under the couches in the living room.

"About three months. I take care of Mrs Lennox while Mr Jeffrey is at work," Mary replied.

Michelle had expected her to refuse to engage.

Emily reappeared.

"Does Mr Jeffrey bring home large items in the middle of the day often?" Michelle asked them both and moved to the hallway closets.

"Mr Jeffrey brings home items of all sizes all the time, but he usually goes directly to his workshop when he arrives," Emily noted worriedly.

Michelle finished in the hallway cupboard and moved to the kitchen.

It was curious that Emily appeared to be willing to entertain the prospect that her boss may have brought home the mace while she wasn't around to see it.

"Emily, can you think of any reason Mr Jeffrey would need a mace?" Michelle posed her question for Emily to be able to answer without feeling disloyal.

"No, Mr Jeffrey spends all his time taking care of Mrs Lennox. When he's not at work he's here with the kids."

As Emily spoke, Mary nodded in agreement.

Through the kitchen window Michelle could see what appeared to be the shed.

"Do you think Mr Jeffrey might have sold the mace for the money?"

The family had two fulltime helpers on an engineers salary. Fredrick and George were adamant everyone knew the mace wasn't worth anything, but that didn't mean someone didn't pay him to steal it.

"We don't know about their finances," Emily advised, and Mary nodded.

"Thanks, Emily. I'm going to have a look in the shed. Mary,

would you mind please checking if Mrs Lennox is ready for me to have quick look around her room?"

Michelle left Emily standing in the kitchen and went out the back door and crossed the lawn. Thankfully the rain had eased.

The workshop was a converted single car garage chock-full of tools, half completed projects and raw materials. It was somewhat orderly but overstuffed.

Michelle noticed immediately that many of Thomas' gadgets were of a similar size to the package in the footage from the tram. James Merrick had remembered distinctly a metal clanging sound. Thomas kept piles upon piles of scrap metal, and tools for working with metal. Michelle saw also that there was packing material which matched the wrapping paper in the footage.

Emily had confirmed Mr Jeffrey brought home packages all the time. Admittedly Michelle couldn't see anything shaped like a crown, but that wasn't particularly compelling. It was hardly a stretch that one, or some, of these items could have been in the package on the tram.

Mary appeared in the doorway.

"Emily says you can come now. But only for a moment, Mrs Lennox is weak today." Mary's nerve returned in defence of her charge.

Michelle had finished checking the enclosed spaces and was satisfied the mace was not concealed in the workshop.

Mary led her to Elizabeth's bedroom on the first floor.

Elizabeth was propped up by fluffy pillows with a scarf around her head. She appeared far sicker than Michelle had expected.

"Mary says you think my husband stole the mace from Parliament. He would never steal anything, ever."

Unintimidated by Michelle's presence, Elizabeth managed to scold her with her diluted voice before succumbing to a coughing fit.

Michelle felt disgusting for sapping precious energy from a dying woman but needed, nonetheless, to search the room.

"Don't mind me, Mrs Lennox. I'm just doing a routine search purely to eliminate your husband as a suspect."

Michelle ducked and peered under the bed.

"We don't need the money, I'm rich," Elizabeth spat, breathless.

Elizabeth might have been dying, but she was still a lawyer from old money. Michelle realised this brave woman did not need her pity.

"If you feel strong enough to speak, Mrs Lennox, can you think of any reason your husband may have been coerced into taking the mace? Blackmail, extortion, anything?" Michelle asked as she opened the wardrobe.

"No," Elizabeth whispered before her eyes closed against her will.

Mary interjected. "She needs to rest, Detective!"

Michelle left Elizabeth's bedroom then swiftly cleared the rest of the upper floor and headed back down the stairwell.

Mary and Emily stood pensively on the landing.

Michelle let herself out.

"He wouldn't do this," Emily called as Michelle walked back to her ride.

Michelle was starting to feel the same way.

# 14

Tamzyn stood at the water's edge and looked out over the Yarra River. Arms crossed, she allowed the pain to flow through her and down her cheeks.

Tamzyn jumped when a figure appeared in the corner of her eye, then realised it was Michelle walking towards her.

"How'd you find me?" Tamzyn asked.

"I wasn't looking for you." Michelle stopped abruptly when she noticed Tamzyn's bloodshot eyes. "I was about to do that too. New career low, interrogating a dying woman in her own bed. You?"

Tamzyn wrapped an arm around Michelle.

"An hour with Thomas Jeffrey. It was brutal. I feel like someone punched me in the soul." Tamzyn sighed. "Thomas says he can't remember what was in the package."

"How convenient," Michelle thought aloud. "There was nothing suspicious in the house or his workshop. They have a fulltime nurse and a helper, but Elizabeth says she's loaded. Assuming she's not lying."

Dying or not, in Michelle's experience, lying to protect family was instinctual.

"Easy enough to check," Tamzyn said. "So no evidence and no

motive for Thomas, and the mace was never at Madame Brussels. So both the tip line leads are out."

Michelle felt numb.

"Back to the drawing board," Tamzyn added.

"Maybe. Do we believe him though? We have a photo of Thomas on the tram with the mace at the exact same time it was stolen. Too many coincidences for it to be a coincidence. Maybe he has a motive, and we just don't know what it is."

When she felt sympathy for a suspect, Michelle pushed herself twice as hard.

"Thomas says he can't remember what was in the package. Who doesn't remember what's in a giant package they carried awkwardly on a tram a week ago?" Tamzyn replied, still bothered by the story.

"Or maybe he never knew. Maybe Thomas delivered the package for someone else and only realised when we turned up that he'd been made an accomplice. That negates the lack of motive."

It helped Michelle that she hadn't met Thomas. Objectivity sharpened her focus.

"Good point. I doubt Thomas would question delivering a package for a colleague," Tamzyn agreed. It was the most plausible explanation for Thomas' blatant involvement in the theft.

Michelle was starting to feel less awful. As she had told Elizabeth, she had genuinely wanted to be able to disqualify Thomas as a suspect. Sometimes her duty challenged her morality but Michelle knew she was doing the right thing, even when she felt repulsed afterward.

"Let's sidebar Thomas Jeffrey for now," Michelle proposed. There were other loose ends that needed ruling out.

"I need my whiteboard. The river is for crying, the office is for brainstorming."

Michelle managed a collegial smile.

They began the walk back.

"Chom got a serve from the Serjeant this morning. He's livid we haven't got any suspects," Tamzyn told Michelle.

"What does the Serjeant care? They're using the old mace?"

Michelle's determination had been ignited by her desire to reunite George with his beloved mace. Otherwise, it seemed a victimless crime.

"Apparently 'public debate is rife with sordid speculation' and 'the longer the mace is missing the more embarrassing it is for everyone involved'," Tamzyn recited verbatim.

"No one is involved. No one has claimed a ransom, no one is affected, and no one knows why the mace was stolen. The Serjeant might just have to suck it up," Michelle grumbled, in no mood for bureaucracy after her morning disturbing Elizabeth.

Tamzyn burst into laughter. "You should tell him that."

Michelle tutted. "Chom can soothe the suits, we've got a mace to find."

# 15

Michelle stood in a rockpool and swirled seaweed with her big toe. Cameron was splayed on a nearby rock.

"I was so furious, honestly, I nearly punched him," Cameron said.

They had been called into Tessa's High School by the principal. It turned out Tessa had been caught kissing Amanda, ironically, in a closet.

"Then I said, so do you call every parent of every student who is kissing someone at school, or have you called me in here to discriminate against my daughter to my face," Cameron fumed, outraged on behalf of his daughter.

"Have you told Tessa?" Michelle asked, relieved her husband hadn't punched their daughter's principal.

"No, I didn't want her to feel embarrassed. She'll tell us when she's ready."

They'd long suspected Tessa had a crush on Amanda.

"I'm sorry I wasn't there. I thought the meeting was going to be about the teacher that quit."

Between Michelle's late nights, Cameron's soccer practice and their alternating chauffeuring of Tessa, they'd barely spoken for more than a few minutes in days.

"I asked about that. Apparently two teachers were having an affair then when their spouses found out they both quit to save their marriages." Cameron laughed. "It was an absurd meeting. I left wondering whether we should find Tessa a new school."

Michelle lay down on the rock next to him. It was nice to have a day with her husband after a fruitless week. When she was making breakthroughs in her cases, the sacrifice was justifiable. When things weren't progressing, she resented the time away from her family.

Cameron ran his fingers through her hair. They had another hour together before dinner with Cameron's sister.

"Are you alright? You don't seem yourself at the moment," Cameron commented.

Michelle had been irritable all week. She was getting annoyed with things that wouldn't normally faze her, like forgetting to buy bread or misplacing her keys.

"This case is just getting to me, nothing's adding up."

"How so?"

Michelle pondered her unease. "I can't find a motive."

"Why not?"

"Because no one benefited from or was disadvantaged by the mace being taken. I can have all the leads in the world, there was just no reason to steal it. Before the mace was stolen, no one even knew what a mace was."

Cameron laughed.

"Maybe it was a public relations stunt for Parliament. Like when a big movie is coming out and the stars have a punch-on in the street the week before the box office opens."

"That's ridiculous." Michelle laughed.

"More ridiculous than Annie's full size replica mace?" Cameron teased. Her laugh filled him with affection.

"I suppose not," she conceded.

It wasn't the worst idea and if exposure was the motive, the theft had certainly worked. The mace mystery was all anyone could talk about. Everyone knew what a mace was now.

"I'm picturing a basement full of scheming historians devising a plan to get the significance of the mace on the front page of all the newspapers," Cameron joked through laughs.

"That may be the most plausible explanation so far. Thank you, my love."

Michelle felt rejuvenated. She needed this time with Cameron. The week had depleted her.

Cameron pulled her into his arms.

"That reminds me, Annie asked if we want to come over for dinner," Michelle said, she had forgotten to extend the invitation.

Cameron sighed. He hated Annie's parties but he would go anywhere to make Michelle happy. "Sure. Why not. Let's take this week from ridiculous to sublime."

# 16

Tamzyn wrote 'Renegade Historians' on the brainstorming white-board in her office.

"Good work Cameron," Tamzyn remarked.

"Take it down." Michelle laughed and rolled her eyes.

"I'm serious." Tamzyn left the note. "We should speak to some historians. Maybe there's something about the mace we don't know."

"Like what?" Michelle replied, willing to partake in some banter as their coffees sunk in.

"George told you the mace is hollow. Maybe there's a treasure map inside."

Michelle nearly choked on her drink.

Tamzyn grinned cheekily and added her outlandish idea to the board.

Chom emerged in the doorway gripping a piece of paper. "Detectives, I have a new lead."

Michelle and Tamzyn responded with applause.

They gathered around Tamzyn's desk and Chom placed the note on the table. It displayed two scrawled names, William Robinson and Alexander Scott.

"I was updating the Serjeant-at-Arms on our progress."

Tamzyn raised her eyebrow.

"Lack of progress," Chom corrected, "and I mentioned we suspected Thomas Jeffrey was covering for whoever asked him to deliver the mace. So, the Serjeant asked around to find out who Jeffrey would help no questions asked."

"Who are they?" Michelle didn't recognise the names from her previous visits.

"William Robinson is a clerk and Alexander Scott is the billiard maker. Robinson's the one who told the Speaker about your visit to Parliament the day before the mace was stolen."

"Why those guys? Because they're dodge or because they need packages delivered?" Tamzyn asked.

"Apparently they're close friends with Thomas Jeffrey. They've all worked there together since they were teenagers."

Michelle didn't want to extinguish Chom's optimism, but the information didn't seem like a lead. "Other than working together, did the Serjeant have a reason to suspect they might have been involved in taking the mace?"

"No," Chom said to Michelle. "But the Serjeant was adamant that if Thomas Jeffrey transported a suspicious package for someone else it would have been one of these two."

Chom turned to Tamzyn for some appreciation but was met with a similarly sceptical grimace.

"It's good to have options," Tamzyn said supportively.

Michelle was less forgiving and pointed to the strategy board. "We can look into it, but I think the bills are more promising."

Michelle and Tamzyn had been working through the bills which had become law the week after the mace had been taken. They had narrowed the possible suspect list down to three matters where an application for an injunction was pending.

Chom inspected the brainstorming whiteboard. He was concerned they were wading into long-bow territory but with the Serjeant-at-Arms and half the state demanding a result, he preferred his detectives to be thorough.

"Alright, what's the plan?"

"We've reached out to the complainants. We're just waiting to hear back," Michelle replied confidently.

Despite the public pressure, the expense of the investigation was quickly becoming unjustifiable. Chom wasn't sure how long he could sustain Michelle and Tamzyn chasing ghosts.

"How'd you go with the second-hand shops?"

"No one's seen the mace. Nothing from the pawn brokers or the silver, gold or scrap metal dealers," Tamzyn confirmed.

"Annie's phone line?" Chom added.

"We cross-referenced the dates and times of the attacks against the sitting schedule. All banal procedural matters, nothing stood out," Michelle replied.

Chom consulted the brainstorming board again. "Why does this say treasure map?"

Tamzyn grinned sheepishly, he didn't want to know.

For all their prospects yet to be discounted, recovering the mace now seemed doubtful. Chom transitioned his outlook from possible to improbable.

"How long until you've exhausted all these avenues?" Chom asked Michelle.

She watched the hope fade from his eyes. He was preparing to give up.

"Two weeks. Three weeks max," Michelle guessed, still optimistic in spite of his withdrawal.

Chom took one last glance at the board and tapped it thoughtfully with his pen. "You've got one and a half."

# 17

John was waiting for Tamzyn on the veranda. It had been a long drive for a quick conversation, but it was worth the trip to strike the Friends of Gippsland off their list.

"I'm John. Samuel's inside," he called as she parked. His expression was hard, but his voice was warm.

"Hi, John," Tamzyn shouted back, taking in the vista.

The Friends of Gippsland had been fighting encroachment into their local native habitat for decades. The scenery was breathtaking.

"I can see why you're so determined to stop this development."

"We're lucky and we plan to stay that way," John said, sounding defensive. "Do you need a break before our meeting?"

"I'm good to go, John. I had a rest in Bairnsdale." Tamzyn followed him into the tin shed.

John Brock and Samuel Myring had invited Tamzyn to meet them at the clubhouse they shared with the local scouts and bowls team. Inside it looked like a sport hall. Tables were arranged in a horseshoe and the walls were plastered with plaques and photos of memorable local sports people.

Samuel was seated at the other end of the hall at a table set with a tea pot, mugs and biscuits.

Tamzyn's research had uncovered that Samuel was the association's founder and president, and professionally an ecologist. John was their volunteer lawyer.

"Welcome, Detective." Samuel stood to shake Tamzyn's hand.

Michelle and Tamzyn had formulated a loose strategy, but it could easily go awry. They were fishing, and Tamzyn had Chom's permission to improvise.

She sat down next to Samuel. "Thank you for agreeing to meet with me during such a challenging time."

"We're grateful for the interest. The decision to proceed with the deforestation was an atrocity. Even the shopkeepers who are usually pro-development got together and raised the funds to lodge the injunction. We didn't even have to ask."

Samuel poured tea for Tamzyn.

"You believe the court will support your injunction?"

The language in their petition had been menacing and Tamzyn had gotten the sense the Friends of Gippsland had been let down by the process far too many times to vest faith in it now.

"We do, we have a strong case. The environmental assessment provided to Parliament was completely inadequate and it provoked a visceral reaction from the community," Samuel explained.

"There were a lot of holes," John added.

"So you don't blame Parliament for allowing the land to be cleared?" Tamzyn asked.

John was cynical of her phrasing and interjected before Samuel could answer. "Detective, before we get ahead of ourselves, would you mind explaining why you're here? You mentioned you're investigating a crime."

Tamzyn had been vague on the phone.

"Of course, John." Tamzyn opened her clipboard and prepared to take notes. "I got in contact with the Friends of Gippsland because we suspected someone was trying to stop Parliament from sitting the week your matter was being debated. The plot was unsuccessful but we're looking for witnesses who saw or heard anyone planning to, shall we say, take matters into their own hands."

Tamzyn seamlessly delivered the intro she'd rehearsed with Michelle.

John gave Samuel a nod indicating it was safe to answer Tamzyn's question.

"No, is the short answer. I don't blame Parliament," Samuel responded. "We use the legal system to block sales, add covenants to titles and lobby politicians. The Friends of Gippsland is mostly professionals. We've been doing this a long time. Sometimes we win, sometimes we lose, but we never stop trying."

"Thanks for your candour, Samuel," Tamzyn said, relieved he hadn't perceived accusations in her query.

"I hope you didn't drive all the way here to ask me one question," Samuel chuckled.

Tamzyn's questions were one of many tools to glean his temperament. Samuel's demeanour was less tense than she had expected.

"Definitely not, I have all afternoon." Tamzyn turned to address John. "I'm also interested in getting a sense of your experience dealing with Parliament. It may help me to identify anyone atypical."

Samuel appeared uncertain about the purpose of the question. John nodded his satisfaction with Tamzyn's explanation.

"Were you in the Chamber when the decision was made?" Tamzyn held her pen poised to record his answer.

"Yes, we have been spectators in the gallery many times over the years."

"And would you say you have a good grasp on how Parliament operates?"

John began to look sceptical.

"Yes, I would say most lobbyists do. It's hard to be effective as an advocate if you don't understand the processes," Samuel replied.

"Indeed," John agreed.

Tamzyn stopped short of asking about the mace directly.

Samuel appeared to be answering truthfully, but something off was niggling at Tamzyn.

"When you were in the gallery, did you see anyone acting strangely or notice anything which seemed unusual?"

"Not that I remember. But, regardless, there's so much security I doubt anyone would have got through the door if they were behaving suspiciously."

"Yes, you're probably right about that, Samuel. Would you mind if I quickly use the ladies?"

Tamzyn excused herself, she needed to distil her intuition.

When she returned, she had reconciled her disquiet.

"Samuel, I appreciate you being so forthright." Tamzyn reached for a biscuit and added casually, "I was expecting you to be angrier. Your submission was very… expressive."

John saw through her performative ease. "What are you implying, Detective?"

"Nothing untoward, John. As I said, I was just expecting Samuel to be fierier, like in his submission."

"It's fine, John," Samuel interrupted willingly. "I find in submissions it's best to forcefully articulate emotion. It's hard to convey how seriously we take our work without some intense prose. I do enjoy writing submissions."

Tamzyn sensed nothing but genuine humility from Samuel. Although, nestled amongst the towering wilderness, she could appreciate the lengths to which someone may have gone to save it. Samuel had revealed his contemporaries would likely have known what the mace was and its role in proceedings. Tamzyn couldn't take the Friends of Gippsland off the suspect list just yet.

# 18

Chom's tenuous suspicion of William Robinson and Alexander Scott was too flimsy to justify summoning them to the station, so Michelle had decided to approach them informally at the parliament building.

Fredrick had begrudgingly provided Michelle with directions, and she made her way to George's workshop to find Alexander Scott.

After Thomas Jeffrey had been interviewed by the police, Elizabeth's condition had deteriorated and he had been granted open-ended leave. As a result, Michelle's presence at Parliament had been met with disdain.

Michelle doubted Thomas Jeffrey's confidants were going to tell her the truth. But if he was covering for one of them, their body language would suffice.

It was clear Alexander Scott had been forewarned that Michelle was on her way. He stood braced at a benchtop holding tools superficially, staring at the door opening.

"Hi, Alexander, I'm Senior Detective Ward. Would you have a couple of moments for some questions regarding the theft of the mace?"

"Not really."

Alexander clutched a handle, his knuckles white from the force of his grip.

Michelle wished George had been in the workshop so Alexander didn't feel ambushed.

"I understand you're friends with Thomas Jeffrey. I'm just wanting to find out if you recognise the package Thomas is holding in this photo. I would ask him myself, but I don't want to disturb his family at this difficult time."

The embellishment suited the information Michelle needed.

Alexander relaxed and let go of his props, then held out his hand for the photo.

"It could be anything," Alexander grumbled, pointing to the array equipment in the workshop.

The element of surprise was ineffectual. Trying to derive any meaning from his hostility was futile. Everyone she had encountered on her way through the building had regarded Michelle with the same antipathy.

"That's all I need. Thanks for your help." Michelle slipped back out into the hall.

Fredrick had described the path from the workshop to the clerk's desk. Michelle walked slowly, avoiding eye contact, observing the behaviour of the staff.

She arrived to find William Robinson assisting a colleague so she tucked herself into an alcove to wait for him to finish.

William Robinson's awareness of Michelle caused him to overtly censor his conversation.

His customer left and William Robinson, in contrast to his colleagues, welcomed Michelle with a broad smile.

"I have been expecting you, Detective. Lovely to meet you. How can I help?"

Michelle was taken aback by his excessively friendly greeting.

"Thank you, Mr Robinson. I was hoping to find out whether you recognise this package Thomas Jeffrey is holding. Obviously, I don't want to disturb him at this terrible time."

William took the photo.

"Please, call me William. He's always taking things home, this could literally be anything." William paused, briefly caught Michelle's eyes, then bent over the counter and whispered, "But it certainly does look like the mace, doesn't it."

Michelle was stunned but his audacity.

"Yes, William. It does."

Michelle left William space to direct the conversation.

"Of course, it couldn't possibly be, but it does look rather like it is," William toyed.

Chom had been adamant William and Thomas were old friends, yet William appeared to be deliberately incriminating his lifelong buddy. Michelle wondered whether the Serjeant's intel had been wrong.

"Do you think it's the mace?" Michelle replied, joining in his bizarre game.

"If it is, I doubt Thomas would have known he had the mace," William speculated playfully.

Michelle felt like she was being conned.

"What makes you think Thomas wouldn't have known?" Michelle asked, exuding intrigue.

"Because he wouldn't hurt a fly, or an ant, or any bug, let alone steal anything," William explained, getting closer to sincerity.

"I hadn't even considered someone else may have asked Thomas to carry the mace. Who would do such a thing?"

Michelle glimpsed a flash of panic before he resumed his witty repartee.

"I was just joking, Detective. Of course it's not the mace. No one here would ever meddle in the affairs of the chamber. It's impossible!"

Michelle didn't want William to realise he'd made a dire miscalculation.

"Of course. I appreciate you helping me with this photo so I don't have to disturb the Jeffreys. I have been so impressed by the professionalism of the staff throughout this whole investigation."

William relaxed and his icky smile returned.

"Thank you, Detective. I'm glad to be able to help. Yes, we've all been through a lot."

"Thanks again, William. We'll have your mace back any day now."

Michelle turned to leave before he could continue his charade.

§

Michelle stood on the steps of Parliament and looked up at its towering columns and allowed the sense of foreboding to wash over her. They were missing something.

# 19

Exford Homestead was one of the oldest residences in Victoria. The acreage and its original buildings had survived largely intact, and Florrie Anderson and Rachel Phillips were determined to keep it that way.

Tamzyn had joined Florrie and Rachel in the windy sunshine as Florrie conducted her lesson, passing down their heritage to Rachel.

Tamzyn had listened intently, mesmerised by the richness of the land's sustained history. Every rock, rivet and fencepost had a backstory.

Florrie had insisted the price of her cooperation was Tamzyn taking the time to understand their fight.

While they walked, Florrie had explained that developers had successfully argued that removing the delipidated barn and blacksmith's forge so they could build townhouses would not compromise the estate's heritage significance. The decision had sent a ripple of outrage through the community. Florrie and Rachel had mobilised the masses and led the campaign to preserve the site.

They arrived back at the homestead and Rachel left to prepare scones and coffee in the parlour for afternoon tea.

The walk was a welcome break from the pressure of the investigation. Tamzyn felt recharged and enlightened.

"I'm glad you enjoyed the tour. Now, what did you want to talk to us about?" Florrie asked, satisfied her side of the bargain had been settled.

"We became aware of a plan to delay your item in Parliament. The plot was foiled without incident, but we are obliged to try and find the culprit. I was hoping to find out whether any of your followers might have been upset enough to take things into their own hands?"

"We did take things into our own hands. We are seeking an injunction."

"I mean pre-emptively, to stop the matter being decided by Parliament," Tamzyn clarified.

"I'm not sure what that would have achieved. If we delayed that would just delay the decision. Why would…" Florrie stopped mid-sentence, realising something foul must have occurred. "I'm being naive aren't I, Detective?"

Tamzyn smiled kindly. "You are not naive, Florrie. But can you think of anyone connected to your campaign who was obsessive or distrusting of a fair outcome?"

Rachel arrived with their refreshments. She had been listening from the kitchen.

"You mean do we know anyone who would have threatened someone to try to get them to vote against the motion?" Rachel said, apparently acquainted with nefarious tactics.

"Something like that, Rachel," Tamzyn confirmed.

The conversation was straying from parliamentary processes but establishing intent nonetheless.

Florrie was alarmed by her protégé's imagination.

"I watch a lot of crime shows." Rachel handed Tamzyn a scone. "It's not poisoned."

Tamzyn laughed insincerely and took the scone, hoping she wasn't about to become a headline.

Florrie afforded Tamzyn a reassuring glance. Rachel had a wicked sense of humour.

"The truth is, we all have our own motivations for becoming involved in the campaign," Florrie explained.

Tamzyn looked puzzled by the comment.

"As I explained on the tour, I believe the heritage significance would be compromised if the site was to undergo any alterations. But some people are interested in protecting the wildlife, others don't want the development next to their house. Others don't want to live through the construction. I can't speak for anyone else."

It was an excellent point, one Tamzyn hadn't considered until now. "I appreciate motivations may vary, but did you notice anyone who was distressed or despondent by the thought of losing?"

Rachel laughed and pointed to Florrie who responded with a weary smile. Tamzyn thought it an odd time to be flippant.

"Rachel's right," Florrie admitted. "I know this land, it's my history. There's no one who cares about preserving Exford Homestead more than me. But time moves on and things change. We used to be surrounded by sheep, now we're surrounded by houses. I'm not unrealistic. My heart broke when we lost, but I understood."

Florrie's voice was heavy with sadness.

Realising she had not helped ease Tamzyn's mind, Rachel added, "Like Florrie said, people around here were mad because the heritage controls were meant to mean something. Exford Homestead is supposed to be significant, not just significant until someone wants to make money. That's what people were really angry about. It was less about what the developers wanted to build, but that they could just change the rules and do whatever they want."

"Do you believe we took things into our own hands?" Florrie asked. She didn't want Tamzyn to leave until the detective was squarely in their corner.

Tamzyn pondered the question. Perhaps someone may have been possessed to meddle, but Florrie had been spot on at the start. Why delay the inevitable? Stealing the mace would only delay the decision, not change the outcome. Also, unlike John and Samuel, they weren't lobbyists. Florrie and Rachel weren't versed in the pressure points of the political process.

"No, I don't," Tamzyn decided and smiled warmly at them both. "Although, I've got my eye on Rachel."

# 20

Chom, Michelle and Tamzyn sat on Chom's couch, deep in contemplation.

The whiteboards were so cluttered with overlapping arrows and question marks that they had become indecipherable.

Waylaid with hypotheticals, the trio were going round in circles.

"We need to start ruling out leads. Tamzyn, be ruthless," Chom instructed.

Tamzyn stood up and positioned herself at the strategy board, eraser primed for the cull.

"Wait!" Michelle jumped up to capture the tangle and took a photograph with her phone.

Tamzyn started with the bills.

"John and Samuel had means but no motive. Florrie and Rachel, possible motive but no means. Remove?"

Chomley and Michelle both nodded and the flimsy leads were erased.

"Two bills down, one to go. Next, Thomas Jeffrey. First, is it the mace in the package? Second, does he know it's the mace in the package? Discuss," Tamzyn tasked, emulating a schoolteacher.

Michelle pursed her lips, feeling anxious from the ultimatum.

Chom squinted at the board. Michelle waited for him to go first.

"It is the mace but Thomas doesn't know it's the mace," Chom suggested to Michelle. She felt like a game show contestant.

"Why," Tamzyn prompted.

"Because William Robinson knows something," Michelle replied. She agreed with Chom's assessment.

Tamzyn erased Thomas Jeffrey's name from the leads and created a new column which she titled 'Patsies'.

"Is the person, or people, who cut Annie's phone line still in the mix?" Tamzyn asked.

Chom and Michelle both nodded.

"William Robinson," Tamzyn posed, arriving at the bottom of the list.

Tamzyn and Chomley looked to Michelle.

"This is what I don't get." Michelle stood up to pace and deliberate. "If William Robinson is such good friends with Thomas Jeffrey, why wouldn't he lie and say he didn't know what was in the package? If he knew it was the mace, and was involved, surely he would point us in a different direction."

Chom and Tamzyn watched with vacant expressions as Michelle stewed.

She continued. "Either he knows it's the mace and is involved, knows it's the mace but wasn't involved or doesn't know anything and is an awful friend."

Michelle felt uncomfortable extrapolating from a brief chat with a conceited gossip.

"We weren't there, it's your call," Chom said.

Tamzyn stood ready to erase William from the leads column.

"Go with your gut," Chom added encouragingly. He was

buoyed by the pace.

"Witness," Michelle blurted instinctively. She didn't think William was involved, just smugly concealing relevant information.

Tamzyn made the adjustment then stood back and recalibrated.

Chom rose from the couch and stood next to Tamzyn and started reconstructing connections.

"If Thomas Jeffrey is a patsy and had the mace in the package, where did it go?"

"He was adamant he couldn't even remember carrying the package, let alone what he'd done with it," Tamzyn agreed.

"It wasn't at the house and Emily and Mary didn't see it. But they also told me Thomas usually takes packages straight to his workshop," Michelle advised.

"Thomas walks home from the tram, so he either dropped it off somewhere or someone picked it up from him," Chom deduced.

Michelle felt her head begin to spin again. The clutter of infinite possibilities returned to rob her of her confidence. Her gut was telling her the same thing it had been telling her the whole time. They needed the motive.

"Either Thomas genuinely can't remember, or he's lying," Michelle replied.

Tamzyn looked concerned. "We can't interview Thomas while his wife is dying. Also I don't think it matters whether he's lying, he's not going to tell us. Like Fredrick said, the staff are like a family. We need another way to figure out where the mace went after the tram."

Chom nodded with reluctant acceptance. Hunger was interfering with his concentration. "Yes, we do. Let's take a break."

# 21

Michelle was seated between a housing developer and a bureaucrat. As etiquette dictated, Annie had set her table for twelve with alternating genders, seating couples as far apart as possible.

Cameron winked at Michelle from the opposite end of the table. Michelle had always wondered as to the purpose of forcing her apart from her husband. She supposed it was to avoid lovers' spats over dinner.

As per Annie's after dinner ritual, the men went outside to the deck and the women went to the living room.

Michelle helped herself to coffee and a homemade chocolate truffle and nestled into an armchair offside the main conversation.

As Annie and the ladies shared stories, Michelle noticed one of the guests staring at her. They had been introduced briefly at the start of the evening. The woman's name was Vida, a headmistress at an exclusive girl's boarding school for the absurdly wealthy. Vida's eyes would dart away as soon as she caught Michelle's gaze.

Realising her curiosity was not as discreet as she had intended, Vida excused herself from her conversation and went to sit with Michelle.

"I'm sorry. I was staring," Vida apologised, embarrassed.

"Not at all," Michelle dismissed graciously. "Have we met before?"

"I don't believe so. I was keeping an eye out for a break in the conversation, I wanted to introduce myself. Annie had mentioned in confidence you're working on the mace mystery. She knows I've been enthralled," Vida confessed, gushing.

The investigation sounded so interesting from this woman's perspective. The reality was not so glamourous.

"I am one of the team," Michelle confirmed with a smile, unable to elaborate.

Vida's face lit up. "It's so lovely to meet you. It's been so exciting following your progress in the news."

The progress in the news consisted of Chom telling the media daily that they had no leads, and nothing had changed, and the media speculating as to what Chom really meant by that.

"I'm glad," Michelle replied, not sure what to say in response to Vida's glee that a crime was proving impossible to solve.

Noticing Michelle's hesitation Vida added seriously, "Don't get me wrong, it's an absolute travesty. We must be the laughing stock of the Commonwealth. I mean, can you imagine what the Queen would have said!"

Michelle almost choked on her chocolate. She hadn't considered the international humiliation which would remain for all eternity if they couldn't find the mace. Michelle hoped the Queen had more important things to worry about.

"Fortunately Parliament immediately reverted back to using the old mace so there was no interruption to the sitting schedule," Michelle assured Vida, feeling obliged to lessen her anguish.

Vida continued unsated, "Still, it's so scandalous. I remember when I first heard the mace had been stolen, I felt furious some-one would dare to play such a disrespectful prank on the seat of power. I was certain it would turn up somewhere silly, yet it never did. It's just such a sinister act!"

Michelle was impressed Vida knew enough about the mace to be offended by its theft. Michelle hadn't come across anyone throughout the investigation who'd been educated enough to be enraged by the incident.

"Who do you think took it?" Vida added as though she was chatting with a girlfriend.

"Unfortunately I'm not allowed to talk publicly about the inves-tigation. But I do enjoy hearing people's theories. Who do you think stole the mace?" Michelle deflected.

Vida clapped her hands with delight and sank back in her chair to think. Michelle watched Vida's brow furrow as she embraced her honorary detective status.

"Well, it has to be someone who works there," Vida proposed, projecting the confidence Michelle was presently lacking.

Michelle smiled. "You sound certain about that, Vida."

Almost all the details about the crime were publicly available. If Vida was following the news as closely as she had portrayed, her speculation was based on the facts.

Vida shrugged. "How else could they have opened the window?"

A bolt of electricity shot through Michelle. She quashed the adrenaline before it showed on her face.

When Tamzyn and Michelle had arrived in the morning the day after the mace had been stolen the window in the Speaker's Chamber had been open. Michelle realised she hadn't considered whether the window was always open or not. Regardless, someone would have had to have ensured the window would be open Friday morning and the only person who had been in the room was the charwoman, Susan Hadly.

Michelle's conversation with Susan had been brief and unrevealing. Susan had said she hadn't noticed whether the locks were broken on the case when she had cleaned the room. However, Michelle hadn't asked Susan about the window.

"Surely the Speaker's Chamber would have an alarmed window," Vida added, vying for Michelle's praise.

Michelle smiled, her pulse still elevated. "Vida, you may have missed your calling."

# 22

Tamzyn had arranged to meet Alfred Sainsbury at his property law practice. Tamzyn had expected the lawyer's office would be modern and sleek. Instead, it was cluttered with mismatched antique furniture.

"I believe you said on the phone that you're looking into a matter at Parliament?" Alfred appeared disinterested in any topic not concerning himself.

"We're following up on a suspected foiled attempt to delay Parliament. I'm trying to rule out parties who are unlikely to have taken matters into their own hands."

Alfred had been representing a row of homeowners about to be displaced by a freeway expansion. Based on his injunction application, the owners believed the road authority had been negligent. It was a battle Alfred's heartbroken clients believed was worth fighting on principle and the hefty cost of his legal bills was an expense they were willing to bear.

Alfred appeared distracted. "You must have a gargantuan number of interviews. There would be hundreds of interested parties in one sitting week, more even."

"We're only following up on matters where there's a time

sensitivity. Such as your clients' homes being demolished," Tamzyn explained. Alfred was obviously across the inner workings of Parliament.

"Makes sense, scarce resources and all that," Alfred said curtly.

Clearly, in Alfred's case there was no motive and Tamzyn didn't have any more questions, but he appeared uncomfortable. Tamzyn's instincts told her not to leave yet.

"How do you think your clients will cope if their injunction isn't granted?"

Alfred's expression sagged. "Most will move on regardless of the injunction. They feel even if this battle is won the prospect of acquisition will always be dangling over their heads. It's just a tough situation. They didn't do anything wrong and their lives have been ruined."

Alfred had gone from looking sad to looking guilty.

"Don't blame yourself. You negotiated a great settlement for your clients. They're lucky to have you."

Alfred smiled, touched by Tamzyn's compassion. Visitors didn't normally realise how intimate property law could be. People's homes were their identity.

Tamzyn watched Alfred churn over his response and waited patiently for him to summon the nerve to say what he'd been suppressing.

"I have to be honest with you, Tamzyn. I was a little taken aback that you're here looking into a delay in the parliamentary sitting week." He paused, courage not quite mustered.

"Really, why is that?" Tamzyn nudged sweetly. She had thought it had been odd that he'd revealed so much private information so carelessly.

Alfred gazed out the window of his quaint office and watched the cars passing, pondering the line he was about to cross.

"There have been rumours for a while that there are… ways one can ensure an outcome."

"Rumours?" Tamzyn queried. Alfred's reluctance to say the word bribery wasn't going to change the reality.

"Inclinations, hints, openings," Alfred bandied. It was not an accusation which lent itself to vagueness.

"Your clients lost their homes. So I take it any openings available, were closed on your part?" Tamzyn asked. She doubted Alfred was going to give her anything else.

"Yes. Of course! I would never jeopardise my reputation," Alfred said loudly, then lowered his voice. "Nonetheless, it's a hard not to feel guilty when people you care about have lost everything."

"Are your clients aware that option was available to them?" Tamzyn wondered in which direction the offer had flowed.

"No. I'm a lawyer not a broker," Alfred said, offended, but the question had needed to be asked.

Tamzyn got the sense Alfred had had no intention of revealing this information before their meeting. His emotions had got the better of him once he'd realised he wasn't being investigated. Tamzyn knew that after she left his office Alfred's charity would rescind. He wasn't trying to be cooperative, he was hoping for salvation.

"Alfred, thank you for confiding in me. It's brave of you to disclose this allegation to a police officer," Tamzyn coaxed, trying to ascertain whether Alfred had anything else to add to his confession.

"Thank you," Alfred sighed and eyeballed one of many antique clocks.

Tamzyn took the hint and stood to leave.

"Your secrets are safe with me, Alfred," Tamzyn assured him. Then she left with more questions than answers.

# 23

Susan Hadley sat in the interview room clad in black. Tamzyn had also attended Elizabeth's funeral. Apparently Tamzyn's conversation with Thomas Jeffrey had meant more to him than she had realised.

Michelle had questioned Chom's decision to bring the charwoman to the station. Michelle, having met Susan, was worried the experience would be traumatising. But they had no alternative. Susan Hadly, however unassuming, was likely an accomplice.

Tamzyn had asked Fredrick to accompany Susan to the headquarters so that he could take her back to work after the interview. She was in no state to drive.

Susan and Fredrick had arrived shortly after the funeral service. Fredrick waited in the hallway.

Michelle and Tamzyn entered the interview room.

Susan was clutching a handkerchief.

Tamzyn had prepared the footage of the entrance to the Speaker's Chamber to show Susan that she had been the only person to enter the morning the mace was stolen.

"I'm sorry to call you in today, Susan. Unfortunately, the conversation couldn't wait," Michelle said.

Susan stared blankly through tears.

"Did you know Mrs Lennox well?"

"Yes, very well." Susan's voice crackled. Her heart broke every time she thought of little Henry, Thomas and Elizabeth's eldest.

"We'll make this quick," Tamzyn assured her and turned the screen to face Susan and pressed play. "As you can see, this is the Serjeant returning the mace to its case after Parliament on the Thursday. This is you cleaning, in and out, on Friday morning and this is Fredrick entering on Friday at lunch time and discovering the mace is missing."

"Detective Ward told me," Susan said to Tamzyn, confused about why she was being shown the tape.

"We just wanted you to see for yourself that you were the only one who entered the room between when the mace was returned and when it was found to have been stolen. We didn't want you to feel like we were singling you out," Michelle explained.

Susan nodded. She hadn't felt victimised but was starting to realise this was not a routine interview.

Michelle continued. "We believe the mace was stolen after you cleaned the room because you didn't notice the locks were broken. As you are aware, the thief used the window to enter the building then pried open the locks and left again out the window."

Susan nodded. She hadn't been asked a question.

"We're wondering whether you can remember if the window was open when you cleaned the room?"

Susan froze. She was too emotionally exhausted to put up a fight.

"We're just trying to find out who opened the window," Michelle added.

Susan was too heartsick to defend herself.

Tamzyn sympathetically tried a different approach. "I assume you've cleaned that office hundreds of times."

"Thousands," Susan replied, still stunned.

"On a normal morning, would the window usually be open or closed?"

Drained, Susan began to sob. "Closed."

"And would you normally clean the window, or open or close the window?"

"If it's dirty I clean the glass. If the room is stuffy I open the window... sometimes but not always," Susan recalled shakily.

Tamzyn signalled to Michelle that they should stop. Susan was clearly distressed.

"One last question, Susan, and then we'll get Fredrick to take you home. On the morning the mace was taken, was the window open or closed when you left the room?"

Susan stared at her hands and took a deep breath.

"I don't remember."

"Thank you, Susan." Tamzyn got up and led Susan out to take her back to Fredrick.

Michelle made some notes and waited for Tamzyn.

When she returned, Tamzyn sat across from Michelle with an uncharacteristically cynical expression and crossed her arms.

"Just because Elizabeth died doesn't mean Susan didn't open the window," Tamzyn blurted angrily.

"What brought that on?" Michelle said, confused. Tamzyn had wanted Michelle to end the meeting.

"Susan can't remember if the window was open. Thomas can't remember carrying a package containing the mace. There are a lot of people who can't remember anything when we need them to."

"The fact that they can't remember doesn't make them guilty," Michelle warned.

"She's an accomplice!" Tamzyn snapped.

"Go home," Michelle said, dismissing Tamzyn sternly.

"Sorry, sorry," Tamzyn apologised.

Embarrassed by her frayed tether, Tamzyn left Michelle to finish the paperwork.

She didn't take offence. Michelle knew Tamzyn was worn thin but her partner was right. Someone was lying.

# 24

Cameron lay beside Michelle, both too awake to fall asleep. They'd been in the kitchen celebrating with Tessa for hours. It was well past midnight.

"How gorgeous was her smile when she told us about Amanda," Michelle said.

"Our daughter is amazing. I don't feel like we did that," Cameron agreed.

"I know its selfish but I'm glad we didn't have more. I want to spend all my time with our perfect one."

Cameron had also been content to stay triangular. Tessa had spent most of her childhood surrounded by her cousins and never complained of wanting a sibling. She liked their small family. Less drama, Tessa claimed.

"We really lucked out." Cameron yawned.

"Go to sleep," Michelle teased.

"No, you haven't told me about your day yet."

Cameron was adamant they debrief every day. Even if only for a few minutes.

"I sent Tamzyn home because she was a mess."

The case had been weighing on them both. There were too

many loose ends.

"Is she all right?"

"We made a few accidental discoveries this week that we should have picked up earlier and I think she's just frustrated."

"Do you feel frustrated?" Cameron asked.

Michelle twisted onto her stomach and propped herself up on her pillow.

"I feel like I'm too experienced to make these amateur mistakes. I'm just disappointed in myself," Michelle admitted. She should have been on to the window from the start.

"It's a lot of pressure. Don't be so hard on yourself."

Cameron always defended Michelle, even when she was wrong.

"I know but every case has its challenges which is why we have processes. I shouldn't have allowed us to be rushed," Michelle argued.

"What's your instinct telling you now?" Cameron asked, he could see Michelle wasn't going to let herself off the hook.

"We need the motive."

"What's Chom's priority? Getting the mace back or finding out who took it?"

Michelle thought about their end goal. It wasn't a distinction they typically made.

"Finding who did it, I guess. Getting the mace back won't solve the crime."

"Does it matter why they did it if you get it back?"

It was almost a philosophical proposition. She thought of George who only cared about the mace's safe return.

"It matters why they did it, so we can figure out who did it, so we can get the mace back," Michelle explained.

"So you need the motive before you can get the mace back."

Michelle felt vindicated hearing him relay to her what she'd known all along.

"Yes, I need the motive."

Chom wanted them to focus on what had happened to the mace after Thomas Jeffrey got off the tram, but she knew in her gut that wasn't going to help.

Cameron stroked her hair.

"Will you go to sleep now?" Michelle pleaded.

"No, I think we should stay up and talk all night," Cameron said with his eyes closed.

Michelle laughed. Cameron was breaths away from falling asleep. "I'm only staying up if you call in sick tomorrow."

"Why?" he grumbled half-heartedly and yawned again.

Michelle turned off the lamp. "Because I don't want you operating a chainsaw when you haven't slept!"

# 25

Michelle was on the phone to Chom who was updating her on the latest tirade from the Serjeant-at-Arms.

Tamzyn popped her head into Michelle's office.

"Annie's here," Tamzyn whispered.

'Bring her in' Michelle mouthed back with a thumbs up.

Annie had never visited Michelle at the headquarters. Michelle felt her nerves surge. She hoped Annie was merely in the vicinity and wanted to have lunch.

Tamzyn showed Annie in and closed the door.

Michelle hung up. "Hello, to what do I owe this pleasure?"

Annie smiled happily and sat down at Michelle's desk.

"The phone lines were cut again yesterday."

Michelle laughed, Annie was glowing. "And you look so happy about it."

"We put up cameras. I have a photo," Annie announced triumphantly, passing Michelle her phone.

Michelle glanced at the culprit. It was clearly Alexander Scott, the billiard maker.

Annie watched the recognition appear in Michelle's expression. "You know him!"

"I do." Michelle smiled and handed back the evidence. "Can I have a copy of this photo?"

"Of course."

"So what would you like me to do about this?" Michelle asked, assuming Annie's visit was a courtesy.

"I thought there was an outside chance it was a spouse. But it's clearly someone you've come across in your mace investigation."

Michelle laughed at Annie blatantly ignoring her question.

"Can you leave it with me? I need to run a background on him to see what we're up against."

"I just want him to stop. Your way or my way."

Michelle didn't want to know what Annie's way entailed. "I'll see if we can figure out why he did it and I'll let you know how we go."

Annie got up to leave.

"Thank you. By the way you were such a hit at dinner. Vida's besotted with you."

§

Chom, Tamzyn and Michelle stared at the strategy board.

"What's a billiard maker?" Tamzyn asked.

"Don't know," Michelle responded.

Chom began stomping around Tamzyn's office wagging his finger at them. "It's got to be connected to the mace. No coincidences."

Chom was fed up with being berated by the Serjeant-at-Arms and his composure was fading.

"I want to go back to the Speaker's Chamber and have a look

at the window again to double check we didn't miss anything," Michelle said.

Michelle had lain awake the night before replaying conversations. Before falling asleep she absolved to begin the investigation again from scratch, applying fresh eyes. The way she should have done from the start.

Tamzyn looked perplexed. "What's that got to do with Alexander Scott?"

"Nothing," Michelle replied. "I just want to get back to the motive."

Chom rolled his eyes. He knew there was no point trying to dissuade Michelle. She had her methods.

Tamzyn walked to the board and drew a wonky diamond linking Thomas Jeffrey, Susan Hadley, William Robinson and Alexander Scott. "What are they all in on and who's the ringleader?"

"And why?" Michelle added.

"Let's haul them all into an interview room together and see what they do," Chom proposed. His plan was both indelicate and uncharacteristically crass.

"I don't want to tip off Alexander Scott. I think we'll find out more if he doesn't know we're onto him," Michelle said.

"Also we don't know if this is a diamond or a triangle. Alexander Scott's phone line-cutting may not be connected to the mace mystery," Tamzyn noted, pointing to the suspects column.

"We've been patient as this lot have continually lied to us. We've got something here." Chom got up and tapped angrily on the board. "It's time to push!"

"Easy," Michelle cautioned. "Are you still committed to a week and a half?"

"Take all the time you need." Chom glared at the suspects list then stormed out.

Tamzyn collapsed into her desk chair. "He's terrifying when he gets like that."

"He's fine. The Serjeant gave him a serve this morning," Michelle explained.

The partners sat in silence, sifting through their own thoughts.

"Why now?" Tamzyn said eventually.

"Why now what?" Michelle replied. She had been thinking about whether she should be looking for one motive or two.

"Why cut the phone lines again now? There were three cuts close together. Then the mace was stolen and nothing. Now the phone lines have been cut a fourth time. So why now?"

Michelle considered the suspect diamond. "They've all been at work the whole time as usual except Thomas Jeffrey."

"And every person we've spoken with thinks Thomas is the nicest guy who ever lived."

"Sometimes nice guys do bad things. We're going round in circles. Do you want to come with me to check out the Speaker's Chamber again?" Michelle asked, keen to get started on finding the motive.

Tamzyn smirked cheekily. "I'll catch you later, I've got a hunch."

# 26

Tamzyn knocked on the giant wooden door of the church. She waited for a minute then bashed on it with her fist. She could faintly hear footsteps and then the door opened.

"Hello, Detective. Did we have an appointment?" the Reverend asked, puzzled.

"We didn't, Reverend. Apologies for the intrusion. I was hoping you might have a quick minute for a follow up question, five minutes tops."

"That's all I've got," the reverend agreed with a hint of annoyance and stepped back from the entrance.

"No need to go all the way to the office, this won't take long."

They sat in the last pew. Tamzyn was aware this was going to be a long shot but she had to try.

"Reverend, we have cause to believe the person who asked you to relay the tip regarding the mace sighting used you to steer us in the wrong direction."

"I highly doubt that, Detective."

Tamzyn had anticipated denial. The reverend was hardly going to accept that he'd been played.

Tamzyn pulled out a folder with the staff ID photos of everyone at Parliament.

"Would you agree, Reverend, that if I can guess who gave you the tip, there's a good chance I'm right," Tamzyn waged.

"I'm not a betting man, Detective," the reverend replied shortly, doubt plastered across his face.

"Humour me."

Tamzyn handed the reverend a card with twelve photos before he could refuse.

"I recognise all of these people. You are aware of that, Detective. You attended Elizabeth's funeral," the reverend admonished.

"I know who gave you the tip," Tamzyn said quickly and pointed to Fredrick Davis.

Tamzyn watched his eyes. The reverend looked reflexively to the photo of William Robinson.

"Detective, I'm not going to reveal who asked me to pass on the tip. I will not risk losing my parishioner's trust. If it turned out the information was inaccurate then I apologise."

Tamzyn didn't need his corroboration. He'd inadvertently given her the confirmation she needed.

"I understand, Reverend. I expected nothing less but we have a duty to ask. I'm sorry to have inconvenienced you. I'm sure you can appreciate we're clutching at straws." She edged toward the exit and slipped back into the sunlight. "Bye and thank you."

§

Michelle stood in the Speaker's Chamber. She stared at the window and ran through every detail again.

The locks on the case had been repaired, the furniture hadn't changed, and frequently used items were in slightly different locations.

The window mechanism appeared to be an original manual fixture. It wasn't alarmed. To open the window someone would have had to have unclasped the metal rod then pushed the window out with their hand, then affixed the frame in place by securing the rod on a knob. Once the window was ajar, anyone outside the building would be able to pull the window fully open to climb inside.

Michelle took out her phone and started to flick through the photos of the hectic brainstorming board.

Elizabeth's passing had thwarted Michelle's ability to gauge the usual temperaments of their suspects. However, after Michelle's brief initial meeting with Susan Hadly, before Elizabeth died, she remembered being left with the impression that Susan was timid and hardworking.

Michelle focused single-mindedly on Susan's motive. Why would Susan Hadly leave open a window for someone to steal the mace? It required planning, coordination, convincing, and courage. The reward would had to have been worth the risk. They'd checked her bank statements and there was no indication she'd been paid.

Michelle stared at the window and said aloud to no one, "Why would a woman who had dedicated her whole life to serving Parliament go rogue now?"

# 27

Michelle burst into Chom's office. "It's the Speaker!"

"What?"

Not following, Chom put down the report he'd been reading.

Michelle raised both arms in the air like she'd just crossed a finish line. "That's the motive. They wanted us to investigate the Speaker. It had nothing to do with the mace. They were trying to get us into the Speaker's Chamber!"

Tamzyn ran through the open door. "It's the Speaker!"

Michelle spun around. "I know. How do you know?"

"How do you know?" Tamzyn repeated, disappointed her thunder had been stolen.

"The mace was stolen from the Speaker's Chamber so we'd look into the Speaker. How did you know?"

"I suspected the tip from William Robinson was a fake to lead us to Madame Brussels. So I went back over the transcripts of what was happening when Alexander Scott cut the phone line and I realised the Deputy Speaker was in charge all four times. I think the Speaker was at Madame Brussels."

"Good work, both of you, but this is a theory," Chom said, quietly proud. "The evidence hasn't changed, we have no confessions, and we don't know what the Speaker is alleged to have done. Most importantly, we haven't found the mace."

Michelle wasn't deterred by the list of obstacles they had to overcome. For the first time, it all made sense.

"I might know," Tamzyn offered sheepishly.

"You might know what?" Michelle groaned. She knew that tone.

"When I met with Alfred Sainsbury he mentioned, off the books, that he'd heard rumours you could buy the outcome you wanted. He didn't go into detail but I got the sense he'd been pro-positioned."

"Are you kidding!" Michelle yelled.

"I'm sorry. I completely forgot to tell you. When I got back to the office Elizabeth had died and it slipped my mind," Tamzyn pleaded, mortified by her oversight.

Chom interjected before Michelle could respond. "Alright, no harm done, we got there in the end."

"Don't use your hostage negotiation voice with me," Michelle snapped.

Tamzyn laughed and Michelle's scowl softened.

"Sorry," Michelle said to Chom.

He gestured for Michelle and Tamzyn to take a seat on his couch. He had been about to call them up to his office before they'd invited themselves in.

"I also have some news. The Serjeant-at-Arms called. Apparently, before she died, Elizabeth engaged a lawyer called George Maxwell to fight to restore her husband's reputation. Elizabeth believed Thomas had been defamed by our investigation and George Maxwell has made so much noise that Parliament has decided to appoint a Board of Inquiry."

"So what? Our investigation is closed?" Michelle fumed, frustrated to be curtailed just as they'd uncovered the illusive motive.

Chom sighed. 'Wife's Dying Wish' had proved to be a potent headline.

"We're getting too close," Tamzyn theorised.

"We've not been shut down yet. Just be mindful we will be asked to hand over the investigation if it's still open when the Board of Inquiry is formed, which will be soon."

"I can't believe this. We finally have a workable theory," Tamzyn complained.

"It's not over until it's over. If you believe in your theory then prove it. Fast."

Chom pointed to the door.

Michelle and Tamzyn left as instructed and took the stairs.

"Good catch with the motive," Tamzyn said.

"You too with the fake tip," Michelle replied, equally impressed.

Tamzyn pondered their diamond of co-conspirators.

"Who do you think we're going to be able to break first?"

"Or should we focus on the Speaker? Try and find something financial?" Michelle suggested.

They exited the stairwell and walked back towards their offices.

"Do you think they took the mace because there was something in the Speaker's Chamber and we missed it because we didn't do a thorough search?" Michelle asked. They hadn't found any personal items.

They entered Tamzyn's office and she set about reworking the strategy board.

"No, I think the staff stole the mace because we went over and saw Fredrick about the phone line and they realised they needed to try a different angle."

Michelle considered the suspects. "And then Alexander Scott started cutting Annie's phone line again because we had missed the connection."

"Makes sense."

Tamzyn added Alfred Sainsbury to the witnesses and moved William Robinson to the suspect column along with Alexander Scott, Susan Hadly and Thomas Jeffrey.

"Say we're right about everything. Why didn't they just call the police or dob the Speaker in anonymously? This web is so elaborate and calculated," Michelle remarked sceptically.

"Maybe they tried and no one believed them. Or maybe they were worried about getting fired."

"Or worse. We don't know what this guy's into," Michelle said.

Tamzyn's eyebrow shot up.

"Annie does!"

# 28

Chom sat in the driver's seat of their surveillance car. Next to him, Tamzyn pointed a long-range camera at the front door of the Speaker's family home. They were both exhausted.

"How long until he's supposed to leave for work?" Tamzyn asked. Her arm was throbbing.

"About twenty minutes," Chom replied, recording the neighbours' movements in the logbook.

There was a tap on the window. Michelle had meant to be there half an hour earlier but her taxi got trapped in a traffic jam.

Tamzyn mouthed 'what-the-hell' then unlocked the door.

Michelle mouthed 'sorry' then jumped in the back seat.

Chom's requests for a search warrant and a forensic audit of the Speaker's bank accounts had been denied. Out of options and time, he had suggested a stake-out. It was dangerous. They all knew how difficult it was going to be to find evidence that the Speaker was corrupt.

"How'd you go?" Michelle asked, trying not to sound too refreshed on the back of a great night's sleep.

"No movement overnight," Tamzyn updated, eye still pressed to the lens.

"No back exit?" Michelle wondered. She was on tonight's shift.

"Not that we can see," Chom replied. "We were talking last night about the motive. You never said how you figured it out?"

"Before we got the lead from the Serjeant that William Robinson and Alexander Scott were involved, Cameron was joking that the theft was a publicity stunt. I realised the evidence had led us to a group of adored, devoted and well-regarded suspects so I thought they probably stole the mace for a noble cause."

"Except for creepy William," Tamzyn refuted. "Now that you mention it, it was a bit convenient that the Serjeant gave us those leads."

"What are you implying? That the Serjeant knew the whole time and was trying to help us, or he's in on it?" Chom asked. It was an outlandish accusation.

"Who knows. Maybe he's as scared of the Speaker as everyone else," Tamzyn said defensively. "Are we supposed to believe of all the employees in the building the Serjeant just guessed two suspects by chance?"

"Let me sleep on it. Literally," Chom replied.

The Speaker's taxpayer-funded driver pulled into his driveway. The Speaker exited his house and jumped into the back seat with a briefcase, then the car sped off.

The undercover team radioed to confirm they'd taken over the tail. Chom and Tamzyn relaxed.

"First night down, how many to go?" Tamzyn sighed.

"As many as it takes, or until we get shut down, whichever comes first," Michelle joked.

"Tools down," Chom instructed in the tone he usually reserved to yell at them. "You two don't have to do this. You have kids and we don't know how deep this goes. All you were assigned to do was find the mace and frankly I don't give a damn where it is."

Tamzyn gave Michelle a nod to speak for them both.

"If we're right, a lot of people put themselves at risk to send us this message. This isn't about the mace anymore. The staff are depending on us. They need our help," Michelle said, respectfully rejecting the out.

Tamzyn slow clapped, quietly. "Couldn't have said it better myself, Partner. Plus, we were detectives before we were mothers. Our husbands knew what they were signing up for."

Michelle laughed, mildly alarmed by the insinuation she was comfortable with risk.

Chom looked unconvinced but admired their determination. He packed up the logbook.

"I'll take your word for it but the offer's staying on the table. If you change your minds, you'll have my full support."

Michelle patted his shoulder. She respected that Chom was responsible for their safety.

"We won't, Boss. But thanks for having our backs."

# 29

Michelle lay on a recliner by Annie's pool, sipping wine. Usually she relished basking in Annie's breezy company but tonight her old friend was distant.

"Is everything alright?" Michelle asked, not wanting to let the tension linger.

"It's been a stressful week."

"Really?"

"Why don't you just ask me what you came here to ask me instead of feigning interest in my business," Annie said, harsher than intended.

Michelle considered denying the accusation but she was there for a favour. Surveilling the Speaker had proven fruitless. If crimes were occurring it was behind closed doors. They needed a different path to the evidence. Annie deserved better than to be fed a lie.

"I was tossing up whether to ask for your help, given you have an interest in our investigation, but I don't want to insult you."

"You know that protecting my clients' privacy is paramount. Our reputation depends on confidentially. But, more importantly, keeping my word matters to me," Annie replied, frustrated that Michelle would consider asking at all.

"Someone deliberately cut your phone line to draw attention to your client because they wanted us to investigate and connect the dots. You're part of this whether you like it or not."

Michelle had tried for compassion but sounded condescending.

"Just because I'm a victim of a crime doesn't mean I'm obliged to join this wild goose chase you've started," Annie snapped.

"All we need is one skerrick of evidence which proves this person is shady so we can get a warrant. We're merely looking for the first piece of the puzzle so we have a chance at filling out the rest."

"How do you know your suspect is my client? Can you hear yourself? You sound completely paranoid."

Michelle grasped at the flicker of hope, not wanting to give Annie more reasons to doubt the veracity of their theory.

"We absolutely know."

Annie watched the pool water rippling in the wind. She put down her wine and perched on the edge of her deckchair.

"How do you know if you can't prove it? Do you understand what you're asking of me? To compromise our values puts my girls at risk. They're not some hypothetical consideration or low value casualties. They're beautiful, wonderful women and they deserve to be shown the same respect as anyone else in your operations."

Michelle was offended that Annie would insinuate she would endanger her staff.

"I appreciate you're worried but we aren't even close to discussing operational details yet. We're the police, every person is equal to us and is entitled to the same protection."

Annie didn't take any comfort from Michelle's disclaimer.

"Exactly. They are as valuable as everyone else and because of their profession you expect them to take unreasonable risks. They will bear the brunt of any retaliation, not you!"

"I hear you, Annie." Michelle was getting mixed messages. "Have you considered that your girls may not be safe now, and that they would be safer if this person was in jail?"

Annie was primed to disagree but was halted by Michelle's excellent point.

Michelle proceeded carefully. "If we could ensure your business reputation is unaffected, and your girls are safe, would you please keep an open mind to helping us?"

Annie mulled angrily. She couldn't sit on the sidelines this time. It was her phone line that had been targeted because someone knew Michelle's suspect was her client. Her girls weren't safe, and she couldn't deny it, and that wasn't Michelle's fault.

"I'm open to a conversation. But not tonight. I'm too upset."

Michelle wanted to leap up and victoriously punch the air but she understood Annie was devastated.

"Thank you. I promise only after we've exhausted every option will we even consider calling on you," Michelle assured her, sad to have compromised the unwritten rules of their friendship.

"If it's what I need to do to protect my girls, then so be it," Annie conceded.

In the past Annie and Michelle had rebounded after tense conversations. But this evening the disquiet remained, and Michelle wasn't sure they could go back.

# 30

George Maxwell had created a fortress around Thomas Jeffrey while he advocated for the Board of Inquiry. Thomas was content to stay at home with his children, still devastated by the loss of Elizabeth.

Tamzyn had convinced Maxwell to allow her to visit Thomas on the basis she was worried about his wellbeing. When Maxwell had checked, Thomas had relayed he wanted very much to see Tamzyn.

When Tamzyn arrived at the house, she almost gasped when she saw him. Thomas had shrunk by half since they'd first met in the interview room. Grief appeared to be eating him alive.

Tamzyn and Thomas sat on opposite couches facing the coffee table. Emily had prepared afternoon tea then taken Thomas' children to the park. Tamzyn was acutely aware she was alone with this broken man in another woman's home.

"How are you coping?" Tamzyn asked redundantly. She didn't have a plan. She was just following her instinct not to wait too long to visit.

"I'm numb mostly. Crying helped at the start, now the pain's just constant." Thomas managed a smile.

"How are the kids?"

Thomas almost flinched at the question.

"They're alright. Emily's been great. When they wake up or go to bed they want Elizabeth, but when they're playing they're in the moment. They can't remember to be sad all the time." Thomas choked on his words, crumpling in front of her.

Tamzyn wanted to go to him and wrap Thomas in her arms but it felt too intimate. Her wedding ring wasn't a shield.

"I'm so sorry, Thomas," Tamzyn said feeling helpless to comprehend his level of grief, and unqualified to offer an opinion.

Thomas pulled himself together to pour the tea and pushed the assortment of biscuits toward her.

"Sorry, Tamzyn. I'm wallowing. Distract me, please. How's the case going?"

Tamzyn froze. She'd had no intention of discussing the investigation, particularly given Thomas was, technically, still a suspect.

"I understand Maxwell is fighting for an inquiry to clear your name," Tamzyn deflected.

If Thomas was an accomplice, a public hearing would draw attention to him unnecessarily.

Thomas looked worn out by the mention of Maxwell. "That was Elizabeth's doing. I can't bring myself to fire him. She wanted him to exonerate me."

"You haven't been charged with anything," Tamzyn noted.

"No, but I'm the only person who had their house searched and, according to Maxwell, if the mace isn't found it won't matter that I'm not guilty because people will always believe it was me," Thomas said evenly.

"It would help if you could remember what was in the package," Tamzyn said before she could catch her tongue.

Thomas frowned warily. "You don't believe me, do you?"

Tamzyn knew the subject was inappropriate but the investigation was unavoidably their connection.

"It's not a matter of belief. You told me you can't remember."

"It matters to me if you believe me," Thomas reiterated, holding her gaze.

"I believe you're a good person and if you were lying to me, you would be doing so for a good reason," Tamzyn replied cryptically, her voice thick against her will.

A shadow of recognition flashed across Thomas' gaunt face and he smiled.

Thomas had more to gain from her discussing the progress of the investigation than the other way around, and Tamzyn quickly changed the topic.

"They must be missing you terribly at work. I met Susan Hadley after the funeral, she was devastated for Henry."

If Thomas noticed her redirection, he didn't show it.

"Susan, George, and some of the others come over every few days to visit the kids. I suspect I miss them more than they miss me."

Michelle had met with George Pearse. He hadn't mentioned he was close to the Jeffreys.

"George taught us about the mace when it went missing. We had no idea what a mace was when we started the investigation," Tamzyn admitted, embarrassed by her ignorance.

"He told me. George and my father shared the workshop when I was growing up. George practically raised me." Thomas laughed, then got emotional thinking about family. "Sorry, I tear up at the drop of hat."

"How about spilt milk?" Tamzyn blushed, realising it was time to leave.

"That too." Thomas smiled longingly.

"I'd better get back to work. It was lovely to see you again." Tamzyn smiled sadly, wishing he was innocent, knowing he wasn't.

# 31

"How are you, Reverend?" Michelle asked. He appeared burdened.

Michelle appreciated the reverend agreeing to meet her, given Tamzyn had accused him of delivering a fake tip.

"I'm fine but your investigation has been testing for many of my parishioners."

"I wasn't aware."

"The uncertainty regarding the thief, and the ongoing media speculation, has knocked them around. They're proud of their work, and many feel the incident has tarnished them all."

"I'm sorry to hear that, Reverend. You might be able to alleviate their discomfort. We suspect some of your parishioners may know who has the mace."

The reverend looked genuinely shocked. "Is that why you wanted to meet with me, because you're about to arrest one of our congregation?"

"No, that's exactly what we're trying to avoid," Michelle assured him. "We were hoping you would help us to encourage the person who has the mace to hand it in to you anonymously. The sooner we can close the investigation, the sooner everyone can get back to normality."

Chom thought the Speaker would be more likely to let his guard down if the investigation into the mace was closed. The shortest route was to find the mace. Michelle had suggested the reverend would be able to encourage his congregation to return the mace. Conversely, Tamzyn had argued the reverend's involvement would alert the conspirators that the police were on to them. It was a double-edged sword but eventually Chom decided the benefits outweighed the disadvantages.

The reverend got up from the table, walked to the sliding door window and sought solace in his tranquil courtyard garden.

"Forgive me, Detective. I'm having trouble with this."

Michelle waited. It was a lot to take in. He returned after a minute.

"So, you don't want to arrest the person who took the mace?"

"If the mace is returned then we can close the case," Michelle said, diplomatically avoiding agreeing.

"Are you certain you know who was involved?" The reverend winced.

"We are. If the mace is returned it will greatly reduce the likelihood we will need to dig further. We have other priorities," Michelle encouraged, pleased with how the conversation was progressing.

The reverend returned to the vista, this time for several minutes.

"If I agree to help you, you will need to give me the names of the people you think were involved. I won't make broad accusations in my church. This is a safe space," the reverend said, stern in his qualification.

Michelle was impressed by how quickly he was able to accept what she was telling him.

"However you wish to proceed, we are grateful for your assistance. If the mace is handed in to you, we won't ask any questions."

Michelle knew in her gut this was the right move. She hoped it would work.

The reverend had paled. "I need some time to speak to my contemporaries and make sure I'm acting in accordance with the expectations of the church."

"Of course. I will use the time to confirm our list of suspects."

Michelle didn't think the reverend was crossing any moral boundaries but was happy to oblige.

"I have been doing this a long time. It never ceases to amaze me the breadth of people's capacities."

"Reverend, without disclosing any details about the investigation, we believe they had good intentions."

The reverend took a long breath, disappointed by the situation.

"Detective, there is never a good reason to steal."

# 32

"It's risky, but is it too risky?" Chom mused, taking the helm at the strategy board.

Michelle and Tamzyn sat on his couch either side of a stack of pizzas.

"I don't see that we have a choice," Michelle replied.

Tamzyn shook her head in disagreement.

Chom had convinced the Serjeant-at-Arms to postpone the Board of Inquiry while the reverend was in play. The Serjeant had agreed to give them a week.

"The second the Speaker gets wind of what we're looking for we'll be shut down," Tamzyn pointed out.

"There's no way Fredrick's never seen or heard anything sketchy," Michelle said, providing the pro to Tamzyn's con.

"And if Fredrick's in the Speaker's pocket we're done. How do you think the Speaker's managed to go undetected all this time? He's got to have people covering his tracks," Tamzyn countered.

After Tamzyn's house visit with Thomas Jeffrey, they'd added George Pearse to the suspects column. Now there were five. Fredrick, however, didn't appear to be part of that posse. It was Tamzyn who'd asked Fredrick to accompany Susan after the funeral.

"When we spoke to Fredrick about Annie's phone line, before any of this happened, he knew about Madam Brussels. He would see who's going where at what time with whom. If there are skeletons, Fredrick's going to know where they're buried," Michelle argued.

"Yeah, because Fredrick did the burying!"

They looked to Chom to pick a side. He wasn't listening to their arguments. He was staring at the list of potential co-conspirators.

"Why do you think they all planned it together?" Chom wondered aloud.

Tamzyn raised her eyebrow at Michelle.

"Is that a rhetorical question?" Michelle asked.

"There's got to be a ringleader but why drag all your mates down with you? They all chipped in and each did a little bit. Why would they do that?" Chom pointed one by one at each of the names.

"Misery loves company?" Tamzyn quipped unhelpfully.

"So that if they got caught they would get lesser sentences?" Michelle offered.

Chom took another slice of pizza, determined not to let hunger derail him this session.

"I doubt Susan Hadley knows how sentencing works," Tamzyn replied.

Chom pointed at Tamzyn. "Exactly. I think they were making sure their plan couldn't get shut down. Someone like the Speaker could just fire anyone who gets suspicious. Like you said Tamzyn, if Fredrick is tipping him off so he stays ahead of the game, perhaps they figured they would be less likely to fail as a team."

Michelle caught Chom's vein. "We thought it was strange the Serjeant plated up William Robinson and Alexander Scott. Maybe the Speaker didn't catch as many of the team as he thought?"

"You think the Serjeant is working with the Speaker?" Chom asked, open to anything.

"Don't know. I guess we'll find out when things start to unravel," Michelle supposed.

"So Fredrick's out. Definitely way too risky," Tamzyn said victoriously.

Michelle awarded Tamzyn a gracious smile in defeat.

Chom moved the pizza boxes onto his desk and sat between them.

"If Fredrick is a lookout and the Speaker gets rid of threats, there's got to be a pile of bodies somewhere. Figuratively."

"Well there's no actual bodies or we'd have heard about it," Michelle joked and got up for another slice.

"Ex-employees," Tamzyn suggested. "But how would we get the records."

"Easy. Just say we got a tip that an ex-employee stole the mace. I doubt the Serjeant would question it," Chom said.

It was a convenient theory but Michelle wasn't convinced. As per her gut, and her tried and tested methods, motive was lacking.

"Sorry to be a buzzkill but this feels like a punt. We don't know what the Speaker's alleged to have done. Based on Alfred's admission, it might be financial." Michelle walked to the board and placed her palm on the co-conspirators list. "Those people are indelibly good. George sees himself as a guardian of Parliament. The Speaker must be doing something to Parliament for them to have felt responsible for stopping him."

Motive first, Michelle told herself again. She knew her process would reward her loyalty.

Tamzyn thought about the goodness of Thomas Jeffrey and blushed.

"Excellent point," Chom agreed. "It's got to be embezzlement. Short of stealing the paintings off the walls, everything else is political."

Michelle felt the fragments aligning.

"The Speaker oversees the operations of Parliament. He would have access to all the bank accounts," Chom added.

Michelle and Tamzyn stared at Chom blankly.

"Do neither of you follow politics?"

"No," they said in unison.

Michelle had begun to feel momentum then reality struck.

"How are we going to solve this in a week? We would need to compare the Speaker's and Parliament's bank accounts, which we can't get. And we would need time for the analysts to find a link, which we don't have."

Tamzyn was standing, hands planted on hips, eyes flitting between her notebook and the strategy board.

"None of our suspects work in accounting or finance. How would they know the Speaker was embezzling? We're missing part of their team," Tamzyn said and turned back to the couch. "If we're going to do this in a week, we need that witness."

Michelle sighed. "The whole point of us going to the reverend was that we were trying not to implicate the staff because it would tip off the Speaker."

"How else can we get a warrant for the financial records? We need a witness," Tamzyn replied.

"Let's look for ex-employees who had access to the bank accounts," Chom suggested.

"Risky, but worth the risk," Michelle agreed. They all stared at the board. "It's the best shot we've got."

# 33

Annie opened her door to find Michelle with a bottle of wine wrapped in a bow.

"I'm sorry." Michelle thrust the bottle towards her.

Annie had been ignoring her calls.

"Sorry you upset me or sorry for what you're about to ask me?" Annie slighted with a forgiving smile. She accepted the wine and let Michelle inside.

"Sorry for upsetting you," Michelle clarified, not wanting Annie to shut the door in her face.

"Do you want a glass of this?"

Annie led Michelle through to the kitchen where she was doing paperwork on the counter.

"No, thanks, I can't stay long. I couldn't sleep. I felt awful that you were angry with me."

Michelle hoped their friendship could survive her misstep. She knew the boundaries and had thus far kept to her side of the line.

"I forgive you but I'm going to try the wine anyway." Annie gathered the strewn papers and put them back into their folder. "How's the investigation going?"

Michelle wanted to ask Annie about the Speaker but she didn't want to reoffend so soon.

"I'm not sure it's worth losing your friendship to drag you back into this."

"As you said, I'm already in it."

Annie picked up her wine, handed a tiny bottle of fancy sparkling water to Michelle and led them out to the patio.

"In that case, I will just be honest about what would help the investigation. But don't answer if it's going to cause a problem between us," Michelle cautioned.

"Double disclaimer, must be bad." Annie laughed, touched by Michelle's high school level bluntness.

"We believe the Speaker is embezzling from Parliament."

"That's a nasty accusation."

"We also think he's a client of yours," Michelle added, not wanting to bluff. They had no evidence.

Annie sipped her wine, waiting for Michelle to ask a question.

"At this stage, whether the Speaker's a client is not the most valuable information to us."

"What do you want to know?"

"We want to know how he pays you."

"Assuming he's a client," Annie teased. She was enjoying Michelle's buttering.

"Yes, assuming the Speaker is a client."

Annie contemplated the road she would be cast upon if she answered Michelle's question.

After Michelle's last visit, Annie had turned the torch on herself. The money her girls earnt at Madame Brussels set them up for the rest of their lives, the connections too. They didn't feel a scintilla of shame. They were businesswomen and they enjoyed the empowerment. But Annie couldn't claim her profession was harmless. Wives were deceived, promises broken, fortunes squandered, all on her watch. Annie considered herself an exemplary business owner and a law-abiding citizen. But when Michelle needed her help, she was confronted to accept that she was neither. She was bound to keep secrets.

Annie sighed, resigned to her conscience. "The Speaker is a client. We have a suite high-profile guests use to meet their mistresses. Like a hotel, but with the required discretion."

Michelle was shocked. She'd not expected Annie to be forthcoming. "So he meets the same woman in the suite?"

Annie felt a strange combination of relief and betrayal. "Her name is Mary Cousins. She's the only woman he sees."

Michelle had struck gold, although she wasn't sure whether Annie's newfound openness came with a catch.

"How does he compensate you?"

"Our regular clients have a tab, they're invoiced quarterly. Sometimes we take a deposit in advance. We've had a longstanding arrangement with the Speaker. He pays upfront in cash."

Michelle was overcome with gratitude but she knew the breach would have been hard for Annie.

"Are you alright?"

Annie looked defeated.

"I'm not sure how much longer I want to do this and I wanted to help you. It was serendipitous."

Michelle couldn't imagine what ambitions Annie held for herself. Her time had always been consumed satisfying other people's needs.

"Congratulations," Michelle said awkwardly, unsure whether this was an exciting change or an ugly end.

"I haven't made any decisions. I don't need the money and my motivation is waning. We'll see."

"Whatever you do, I hope you keep having dinner parties."

Annie smiled. She looked like she'd made up her mind but not realised it yet. She needed reassurance her sacrifice had been worth it.

"Will this information help solve your case?"

They were getting closer, Michelle could feel it.

"Absolutely."

# 34

Chomley had expeditiously secured the staff profiles of all the ex-employees from the past decade. Turnover had been low and the last person to leave the accounting team was two years prior.

Robert Clark had been second-in-charge when he had retired after sixteen years of service.

Tamzyn wasn't sure what to expect, but it was clear once she'd arrived at his local that Robert spent more time at the pub than at home.

Tamzyn ordered him a pint and a soda water for herself, and they found a secluded booth.

"I have to admit, Robert. I have an ulterior motive for this meeting."

Tamzyn had told him they needed him to verify some documents associated with maintenance of the mace which bore his signature.

"No records?" Robert replied, disappointed.

"Sorry, no records. We have reasons to believe someone in the building is embezzling. We were hoping you would be able to help us figure out how they might be doing it."

It was an utterly unreasonable request, but the Serjeant's deadline was looming and they were running out of time.

"Why me?" Robert asked.

Tamzyn had been expecting Robert to react cagily and was ready to launch into a reassuring monologue but he didn't seem bothered by Tamzyn's admission.

"We're concerned that if we ask a current employee, they might accidentally alert the suspect."

Robert beamed. "This is so exciting! When do I start?"

Tamzyn almost burst out laughing.

"If everyone we asked for help was so accommodating, Robert, my job would get done a lot quicker."

Tamzyn relaxed.

"No one tells you how boring retirement is. I probably would have stayed working forever if I'd known. Of course, I couldn't have. The wife would have killed me," Robert declared, chuffed to be useful.

"We can start right now if you have the time?"

Robert laughed and waved his arms around, alerting Tamzyn to their leisurely surroundings. "I have the time!"

Tamzyn laughed as she pulled out her clipboard and a pen.

"Great, let's just have a conversation and see where it goes," she suggested. She didn't know what she didn't know.

"Okay." Robert rubbed his hands together in anticipation.

Tamzyn went in hard. "If you were going to steal money, how would you do it?"

Terrified of getting the answer wrong, Robert panicked. "I'm sorry, I don't have a devious mind."

Tamzyn was touched by Robert's virtue and inverted her query. "No worries, that's completely understandable. What safeguards are in place to stop people stealing money?"

That answer Robert knew and he lit up.

"We had very strict auditing and double verification sign off requirements."

Robert may as well have been speaking a different language.

"Would you mind please explaining in detail how those deterrents worked?"

"Auditors come in every year and check all the account entries to make sure the details add up and all the information that is required by law is recorded." Robert waited for Tamzyn to finish writing her sentence then continued. "Double verification means that two people need to sign off on everything, there is no one person responsible for approving payments. Then there's all the normal computer stuff, like passwords."

Tamzyn scribed furiously, trying to capture all the important elements of his explanation.

Robert looked very pleased with himself and took a celebratory swig of beer.

Tamzyn digested the measures.

"So if two people were in on a scheme they could bypass the double verification and steal the money and split it?"

Robert reverted to muscle memory. "Theoretically, but the auditors could still pick up anything suspicious and the money would still have to come out of someone's budget. The manager would probably notice if their allocation was impacted."

"So there would need to be a lot of people conspiring in order to pull off a heist?"

Robert laughed. "Except there's no one in my team who would do it. I'm sorry, Detective. I know them, they just wouldn't. They're good people."

Tamzyn appreciated Robert's steadfast positivity. Her job, however, required perpetual and unbiased application of doubt.

"What about mistakes? Surely the auditors found errors. Dots in the wrong place, too many zeros?"

Tamzyn felt guilty for tarnishing this chirpy man with her cynical brush.

"Yes, often. Mostly information that was missing, incorrect allocations, processes followed improperly, that kind of thing," Robert explained, enjoying reminiscing.

"What's the worst mistake the auditors ever found?" Tamzyn pressed, determined to find the weak link.

Robert folded his arms and stroked his chin in what Tamzyn could only assume was his thinking pose.

Eventually he started laughing and smiled.

"One year we paid a staff member her salary for eight months after she had retired. The paperwork never got to us so we never cancelled the automatic payment. She didn't realise because she was living off her superannuation and her salary went directly into a long-term savings account. We only realised when she called and told us." Robert chuckled at the memory. "I shouldn't laugh, it was mortifying at the time. She mailed us a cheque for almost one hundred thousand dollars."

"Were the accounts audited within that time?" Tamzyn asked, a glimmer of hope emerging.

"I believe so. They didn't pick it up. The payment was in accordance with the paperwork. The paperwork was just wrong."

"Robert, this really is excellent information. I can't thank you enough. One last question, what's the maximum amount for a cash payment?"

Robert had to think about it, he was fast on his way to sloppy. "Unless its changed, I believe back in my day it was $100."

Tamzyn had more than enough, and so had Robert.

# 35

Tessa was shredding lettuce and radish for the rice paper rolls. She had already recorded this recipe and Michelle was looking forward to an actual conversation.

"How are things with Amanda?" Michelle asked.

Cameron had mentioned Tessa had been a bit quieter than usual. Michelle felt guilty that she hadn't noticed the change and was determined to get to the bottom of her daughter's malaise.

"Alright." Tessa shrugged.

"You don't look very sure about that?" Michelle coaxed affectionately.

"We're good." Tessa sighed heavily then added. "We never used to fight and now we fight all the time."

"Fight about what?"

Michelle couldn't imagine Tessa and Amanda arguing.

"Everything. Little things, big things. Jealousy mainly."

Michelle almost laughed. They'd been at school with the same people for a decade, she couldn't imagine who it could be.

"Who's jealous, you or Amanda?"

"There are a few people who like me. I keep telling her there's no one else I want to be with. She knows it's stupid. She wasn't this emotional when we were just friends."

Michelle was secretly amused Amanda was the one who was lovesick.

"Do you want to go back to just being friends?"

"No." Tessa blushed.

Michelle felt fortunate Tessa was still living at home when she'd fallen in love for the first time. It was a gift to discover a new dimension to her daughter.

Done with her confession and the lettuce, Tessa moved on to grating carrot. Her temperament, however, hadn't changed. She was still downbeat.

"You don't seem yourself. Is something else going on?"

Michelle wasn't going to let it go, her maternal self-esteem hung in the balance.

"I'm just worried about you."

Michelle was blindsided.

"Why on earth are you worrying about me? I'm the adult around here."

"The mace mystery is just really awful."

Tessa had never commented on the impact of Michelle's work before.

"Why?" Michelle asked, clueless as to where Tessa was getting these ideas. Certainly not from her or Cameron.

"They were saying on the radio this morning that a Board of Inquiry has to take over because the police are too stupid to solve the crime. And it's on the news every night, and people at school are saying the detectives must be incompetent. It must hurt."

Michelle stopped slicing the ginger and went around to Tessa's side of the bench.

"I'm completely fine. We're sheltered from all that. Chom deals with the media, and the politics, and Tamzyn and I just get on with the work. We can't tell the public everything or it would jeopardise the investigation. Those people on the radio would have no idea how we work or what we know," Michelle said, devastated her daughter had been needlessly suffering on her behalf and she hadn't realised.

Tessa's face brightened. "So this might be over soon?"

"The Board of Inquiry will take over next week, but I don't want you to worry about that. Are you eavesdropping or are people being rude to you at school?"

Michelle could see Tessa was considering lying to spare her mother's feelings. Fortunately, Tessa chose honesty.

"A few people, but it's fine. They aren't my friends. I don't care what they think."

"You don't have to put up with bullying. I can call the school or we can find you a new school."

"No! Mum, I'm fine." Tessa smiled. "I was just worried about you. But you don't even care."

"I care people are being mean to you."

"They aren't being mean. They're just trying to find out what's going on with the case. I'm like a celebrity at school now. It's weird. I tell them you don't talk about work at home but they don't believe me."

"Maybe we should send Chom round to the school to corroborate your story." Michelle winked.

Michelle realised why Amanda was jealous, she was used to getting all the attention.

"Please don't." Tessa giggled.

Michelle sighed with relief. She might not be able to solve the mace mystery, but at least she was able to solve the mystery on the other side of the kitchen bench.

# 36

Alfred sat with his back pressed against an antique chair, arms crossed, glaring at Tamzyn.

It had taken superhuman powers of persuasion to convince him to let her back inside his office.

"I knew our conversation would come back to haunt me. What happened to 'your secrets are safe with me'?" Alfred spat.

Tamzyn regretted not bringing Michelle but then Alfred definitely wouldn't have agreed to see her.

"I'm not haunting you. We just need your help. This is begging," Tamzyn refuted, aware the semantics were not his issue.

"What do you want?" Alfred grumbled, no sign of defusing.

"We need to get our hands on Parliament's financial records. We can't get a warrant because we have no evidence. We were hoping you would give us a statement to say that you had been offered a deal."

"Absolutely not. Why would you even ask me? I made it crystal clear when you were here before, I want no involvement."

Alfred had begun to quiver but he hadn't thrown Tamzyn out yet, which she chose to interpret as a good sign.

"Alfred, we never would have known what was going on if you

hadn't courageously spoken up."

Tamzyn wasn't above resorting to flattery.

"Why are there no people connected to your case who can help you?"

Alfred's anger started to subside as the lawyer in him kicked in.

Tamzyn knew his cooperation hinged on this answer. She couldn't say 'because everyone is too terrified to talk to us' or she'd lose him.

"The truth is, we have a mole. We don't know who we can trust and I know I can trust you."

Tamzyn embellished their situation with Fredrick. It was a stretch.

Alfred resisted a smile but the knight in him wanted to rescue the damsel.

"We ask the wrong person and the whole case is shot," Tamzyn pleaded. "Alfred, you're our only hope."

"Doubtful. Can't you get a hacker or something?" Alfred's tone betrayed him, Tamzyn had a hook in.

"We can't. We need to do everything by the book, or we won't get a conviction."

"I'm not saying yes, but what do you actually need?" Alfred shook his head at Tamzyn's pout. He was fully aware he was being manipulated but was enjoying the spectacle.

"We just need a statement saying you were offered the opportunity to pay for a favourable outcome in your matter. It won't have to name anyone and you'll remain anonymous to everyone but the judge. We just need you to write a letter."

They had debated for hours in Chom's office whether a witness account from Alfred would be enough to compel a judge to give them a warrant to access Parliament's financial accounts, but they decided it was worth a shot.

"Am I in danger?" Alfred asked meekly. The effect of Tamzyn's performance was wearing off.

"Not at all. You aren't connected to our case in any way. No one outside of my partner and my boss even knows we spoke to you. To be honest, I actually forgot to record the details of our meeting because I had to attend a funeral," Tamzyn admitted, hoping to reinforce how unfindable he was.

"I'm sorry for your loss," Alfred said, sorry but relieved.

"Thank you. It was a rough week." Tamzyn smiled appreciatively.

"Even if I did agree to help you, my statement would be flimsy. Rumour and innuendo. Anything I've experienced could be explained away as circumstantial."

"I understand your reservations but we just need to get a warrant so we can find the hard evidence. We think the fact that you're a lawyer will get us over the line."

Tamzyn was willing to sit there all day and rebut his concerns.

Alfred left the desk and began to pace while he considered the implications.

He crossed his office a dozen times.

Tamzyn dared not disrupt his internal deliberation.

"I will write the letter for you. But I will not attend a trial or serve as a witness unless forced by the court," Alfred said, feeling gratified and weary. "I am many things, Tamzyn, but a coward isn't one of them."

Tamzyn jumped out of her chair. "Alfred, thank you. You have no idea how much this changes things for us. How can we ever repay you?"

Alfred smiled, amazed at himself for being charmed by her theatrics. "Once you have your warrant, lose my address!"

# 37

Michelle watched Tamzyn hurtling down the hallway. Fortunately the door was open and Tamzyn grabbed the architrave and flung herself into Michelle's office.

"The reverend wants to see us at the church," Tamzyn wheezed.

"Does he have the mace?"

"Don't know."

Michelle was perturbed by the suspense. "What does the bible say about taunting?"

"Get up!" Tamzyn yelled excitedly, waving her arms about, car keys in hand.

Michelle gathered her essentials. "This had better be worth the trip."

§

"I think I'm going to throw up," Tamzyn whispered, her heart in her throat.

Michelle shot her a look to calm down and slammed her fist on the door of the church.

An assistant arrived to let them in and they proceeded to the reverend's quarters.

Michelle grabbed Tamzyn's arm to stop her from running through the church.

Tamzyn sighed. "If the mace isn't in there, I'm going to cry."

Michelle laughed and knocked on the door.

The wait was agonising.

"Come in," the reverend called.

"Here goes." Tamzyn turned the handle and pushed.

The Reverend sat behind his desk. The mace lay on top of his paperwork.

Tamzyn gasped and Michelle's eyes welled. Relief and exhaustion combined, they were too awestruck to speak.

"I haven't touched it. The mace was there when I arrived this morning."

"Do you know who returned it?" Michelle asked.

They'd already agreed in writing to the amnesty, she was just curious.

"No. I spoke with everyone on your list and told them I would leave the sliding door to the courtyard unlocked until the mace was surrendered anonymously," the reverend revealed, proud of his strategy, disappointed in his flock.

"Can I touch it?" Tamzyn said to Michelle.

The reverend laughed. "I'm not sure how else you're going to get it out of here."

They had promised not to fingerprint the mace upon return. Michelle took some photos of the desk then nodded to Tamzyn to proceed.

Tamzyn crept towards the mace like it might bite her then stroked the crown before she picked it up. She'd stared at its picture a million times, dreamt of countless scenarios in which the mace would find them.

"It's lighter than I thought it would be," she marvelled.

Michelle had never been so happy to recover stolen property.

"We've been looking for you," Tamzyn cooed to the mace.

The reverend and Michelle shared an amused glance.

"It's been a long investigation," Michelle said, shaking from the adrenaline.

"Do you have a bag?" the reverend asked, noting they were empty handed.

They didn't. Michelle's professionalism kicked in.

"Reverend, we will need to consider when to tell the public the mace has been recovered. Have you told anyone yet?"

"I haven't. I called Tamzyn as soon as I arrived, then cancelled my meetings for the morning. None of my staff have been in the office. I'm the only one with a key."

Michelle's mind was racing. The Board of Inquiry was set to commence any day. If they announced the mace had been returned, it would be conspicuous if they kept poking around Parliament.

"Reverend, given the crime was not solved, we need time to consider how to manage the optics. Do you mind keeping this to yourself?"

Tamzyn cradled the mace, watching her partner command the situation.

"Whatever you need, Detective. Please keep me informed so I can forewarn the church of my involvement. We will also need to manage perceptions."

He wasn't naive. The media would discover someone connected with his church had committed the crime eventually.

Michelle nodded. It was a win, win, win.

"Reverend, do you have a blanket I could wrap around the mace, please. Our duffle bag is in the car. We didn't want to be presumptuous," Tamzyn lied.

"I'm sure we can find something."

The Reverend left them in the office while he searched for a suitable covering.

Tamzyn snuggled the mace. "Best day ever!"

# 38

Thanks to a statement from Alfred, and a lot of convincing from Chom, the judge had finally allowed them access to Parliament's financial records. The forensic police accountants had one copy in their lab and Michelle had the other.

Tamzyn had invited Robert to help look for abnormalities and the four of them sat in Chom's office pouring over spreadsheets.

"This is hopeless," Tamzyn declared, throwing her hands up in the air.

After Robert's introductory lesson on how to audit accounts, they'd quickly got the hang of reading the bank statements and balance sheets.

"Keep at it," Chom encouraged. Impatience and frustration were getting the better of all of them.

Relishing the action, Robert chimed in. "Look for unusual descriptions or repeated items with no references."

Tamzyn needed a break and moved to the window to look out at the water to rest her eyes. "Even if we can find a discrepancy in the accounts, we know the Speaker pays Annie in cash."

"Who's Annie?" Robert asked.

"Just a friend who gave us a tip," Michelle replied.

After the mace had been returned, Michelle's motivation had surged. She wasn't leaving Chom's office until they found something incriminating. She'd warned Cameron it would be an all-nighter, or two. She also needed to keep guard, they'd hidden the mace under Chom's couch.

"It would be difficult to withdraw cash without drawing attention to yourself. Cash isn't used to pay creditors, ever," Robert said.

"We know the Speaker makes at least one large cash payment quarterly. They could space out the withdrawals in smaller amounts in between?" Michelle suggested.

Robert shrugged, accepting he didn't have all the details and continued examining a balance sheet.

Tamzyn apologised as she sat back down, pessimism was lethal. "Attitude adjusted. We can do this!"

Michelle laughed and they got back to work.

They broke for dinner, then broke for a walk and then broke for a snack. Michelle was about to concede she needed to go home to sleep when she spotted something in one of the maintenance bank accounts.

"Mary Cousins. Does a staff member by the name Mary Cousins ring a bell for you?" Michelle asked Robert.

"No, but I haven't worked there for years. Might be someone new."

Chom and Tamzyn kept working.

"Same name as the Speaker's mistress. Coincidence?" Michelle reminded them.

"Unlikely," Tamzyn said.

"What's the entry?" Chom asked.

"The description says Monthly Salary Maintenance Special

Projects Team and the payment is twelve thousand," Michelle read.

"Annual salary of one hundred and fifty thousand. Not too shabby," Tamzyn calculated.

"So the Speaker's sleeping with someone at work?" Chom queried, not following.

"I don't think Mary works at Parliament. Annie said she's a fashion designer."

Robert scowled at Michelle's screen.

"Did you find something?" Chom asked Robert.

"I don't remember a Special Projects Team in the Building Maintenance Department."

"It wouldn't be hard to confirm," Tamzyn noted.

Michelle pursed her lips. "Robert, is there a way to narrow the records to show only the transactions relating to the Special Projects Team?"

"Sure, give me a minute."

Robert's hands flew across the keyboard as he worked.

"What are you thinking, they fudged the books?" Chom asked Michelle.

"Unless it's a different Mary Cousins, how would they get the expense past the manager? Surely someone would have noticed a gaping hole in their budget."

"Here you go." Robert swivelled the screen. "Looks like about ninety thousand worth of payments per month for just over a year and a half."

"That's like, one and half million dollars," Tamzyn multiplied loosely.

Michelle studied the screen. "The descriptions are pretty vague. If I hadn't recognised Mary Cousins' name I would have looked straight past this."

"Robert, how likely is it that the Special Projects Team could be a rort, given all the safeguards?" Chom asked.

Robert scanned the entries he'd collated. "All permissions are done electronically. To be honest, it would probably be easier to fake a whole team than one person."

Michelle gasped and Tamzyn looked astounded.

"You think the Speaker invented the whole team?" Chom replied.

"I don't think anything. It would just be easier, procedurally, to invent an off-site team that did all their paperwork electronically and remotely than it would be to invent one person who reports to a manager for a job they don't do."

"I'll give forensics a call." Chom slapped his comrade on the back. "Good work, Robert."

Robert beamed at the officers, he was in his element.

"Happy to be of service."

# 39

"That's her," Annie confirmed as Michelle held her phone camera up to the one-way mirror.

Mary Cousins was draped in a glamourous dress with irritation etched around her eyes. She tapped the toe of her impossibly high heel shoe against the table leg.

"Does she know why she's there?" Annie asked sympathetically.

"We had a patrol car tail her. She ran a red light. She didn't realise no police officer would ever bring you back to the station to book you," Tamzyn replied cheekily.

"We'd better get going," Michelle said to Annie.

"Good luck," Annie said then hung up.

"She looks like a mistress," Tamzyn thought aloud.

"Don't be judgemental," Michelle scolded.

Michelle switched on the recording equipment and they moved around to the interview room.

Mary was confused by the change in personnel. "Who are you?"

"I'm Senior Detective Ward and this is Detective Nixon."

"I admitted I ran the red light. I want to pay the fine and get out of here. No investigation required," Mary mocked rudely.

Tamzyn rarely had adverse reactions to suspects but she disliked this woman. Mary was as obnoxious as the shimmer all over her face.

"We would like to talk to you about your boyfriend," Tamzyn said, containing her disdain.

"What about him?" Mary replied, neither surprised nor abashed.

They'd discussed at length how to approach the interview. It was Chom's view that they had nothing to lose. The mace was back, the Board of Inquiry was about to take over the investigation and he wasn't scared of the Speaker. Michelle had his permission to leave all their cards on the table.

"We think he's using your identity to steal money," Michelle said.

Mary pursed her lips sceptically.

"He's stealing my money? Why would he do that, he has his own money?"

Michelle was amazed Mary continued to answer their questions. They had no way to keep her at the headquarters if she wanted to leave.

Tamzyn produced a paper bank statement and pointed to a transaction carrying her name.

"See here. Do you work in maintenance at the parliament building?"

Robert had helped them to confirm though a friend on the current staff that there was no employee named Mary Cousins and there was also no Special Projects Team.

Mary looked appalled. "Do I look like a cleaner?"

Tamzyn and Michelle exchanged an amused glance, she clearly had no idea what was going on.

"Mary, we checked the bank account on the other end of this transaction. Is this you?"

Tamzyn showed Mary a copy of a bank's application form with a picture of her driver licence.

The heavy makeup stuck to her face, but the arrogance disappeared.

"That's my licence. Am I in trouble?"

"Have you done something wrong?" Tamzyn replied curtly.

Michelle shook her head slightly at Tamzyn. They couldn't afford to alienate her. They needed Mary's cooperation. "Mary, you aren't in trouble. It must be painful being in love with a married man."

Mary looked resigned as opposed to sad. "Most of the time I'm fine."

"And you're okay with fine? You don't want more? Family home, wedding ring?" Michelle added gently.

Mary talked to Michelle and ignored Tamzyn. "I can't marry him, he's got responsibilities. It's not something I think about anymore. What we have is real love, that's enough for me."

Michelle could feel Tamzyn twitching beside her and kicked her under the table.

"Mary, I'm married. My husband would never put my name on a bank account without telling me."

"Maybe he was trying to put some money away for me," Mary suggested desperately.

"Do you believe that, Mary?" Michelle said as delicately as she could to bring Mary back to the issue of fraud.

Mary didn't answer. She just stared at the table, clearly thinking about something.

Michelle wanted to let her go before Mary realised she didn't have to be there.

She nodded to Tamzyn to deliver the blow.

"Mary, I'm sorry to be the one to tell you this, but your boyfriend has stolen over 1.8 million dollars in your name. And that's just what we know about. If you aren't involved, this is your chance to talk to us."

"She's right, Mary. This man isn't your husband. It's likely he'll go to jail for a long time. You can start over and find a nice guy who isn't going to treat you this way."

Mary didn't respond. She was in shock.

"Mary, this is my card. Have a chat with your lawyer and let us know in the next few days what you want to do." Michelle stood up. "You're free to leave."

"But I didn't pay the fine for the red light," Mary choked foggily, tears starting to stream.

"We'll waive it for you this time, Mary." Michelle patted her hand. "You've had enough bad news for one day."

# 40

The Serjeant-at-Arms had led the Speaker from Parliament amidst a blaze of camera's flashing. The Speaker just shuffled along. Resigned, like Mary, to a life according to someone else's timetable.

Shortly after the arrest Chom announced the mace had been recovered. In the shadow of the Speaker's downfall, the reporters who had hounded him relentlessly had barely noticed that its robbers had evaded justice.

Tamzyn knocked on Michelle's office door. Michelle was creating a chronology. The details floating around in their minds needed to be committed to record for the courts.

"George is here to pick up the mace," Tamzyn advised, feeling tired to her core.

"Great, can you bring him in, please?" Michelle asked. She was in the middle of a half-formed sentence.

"Sure," Tamzyn said, she needed a break anyway.

"Don't tell him we hid it under the couch," Michelle called after her.

Tamzyn stuck her thumb in the air and kept walking.

Parliament had been granted an exemption to allow for the mace, which was technically still evidence, to be returned to continue its service to the state. After the press conference where Chom had waved it around to prove they'd really got it back, he'd entrusted Michelle to see the mace home safely. Secretly scared she'd break it, Michelle had asked George to pick it up himself.

The mace sat on Michelle's windowsill in a duffle bag, crown poking out, still partially wrapped in the reverend's blanket. It looked profoundly misplaced but was nonetheless magnificent.

Tamzyn returned with George and the case. He gasped then laughed when he saw his precious mace in such undignified surroundings.

Tamzyn left them. She'd already said her goodbyes to the mace, much to Michelle's horror and amusement.

"Detective, thank you." George placed his hand on his heart.

"We didn't want to scratch it, but it doesn't fit fully in the blanket," Michelle apologised, feeling embarrassed she'd not afforded the mace greater respect.

"I'm sure you did your best."

George lay the case over the arms of the chair opposite her desk, carefully pulled the mace out of the blanket and rested it back in its moulding.

"Do you need to inspect it?" Michelle asked, surprised he didn't take a thorough look.

"No, it will go straight to our conservator. They will document and repair any damage." Emotion seeped into his words, he was overcome. "I thought I'd never see it again."

George's hands shook as he buckled the new clasps and secured the new locks.

With the speed at which the dominos had fallen once Mary had turned on her boyfriend, Michelle had forgotten that they'd assigned George to the suspects column. Seeing him in this state however, it was clear he'd not been involved. Or at least didn't know where the mace had gone after its ride on the tram with Thomas Jeffrey. Michelle wasn't going to ask. George had been through enough. She was content not to know, and perhaps never know.

"George, thank you for your help. If you hadn't taken the time to explain to me why the mace was so important, I may not have tried so hard to get it back for you," Michelle admitted sincerely.

George blushed. "Always happy to talk about my work to anyone who will listen."

"How's everyone coping after the arrest?" Michelle asked.

"Shocked but mostly relieved it's over. Living under a spotlight was challenging. Trying to grieve Elizabeth with Maxwell all over the news has been… less than ideal."

Michelle hoped for all their sakes the Board of Inquiry would be forgotten when the politicians found something else on which to fixate their performative outrage.

"It has been an honour working with you," Michelle said, full of gratitude.

George picked up the case, eager to get the mace home safely.

"Do come and visit us again, Michelle. Next time under happier circumstances."

# 41

Michelle had collapsed on the couch and Tessa had taken the helm preparing tacos for dinner.

Michelle slumped, sans thoughts, and listened to her daughter pottering around the kitchen. Even the sounds of Tessa cooking were more confident. Between becoming a minor celebrity and the love of a good woman, Michelle was starting to see glimmers of the adult Tessa would become.

Cameron finished cleaning his tools and joined Michelle on the couch. He'd seen the arrest on the news and lent over and kissed her.

"Congratulations. Now I know why you've been so busy this past week."

"Thank you, a week that felt like an eternity."

"I'm so proud of you." Cameron kissed her again.

"It was a team effort," Michelle said, warmed by his praise.

"Are you alright?" Cameron asked.

Michelle didn't seem joyful like she normally did after she closed a hard case.

"I'm just tired. There were a lot of people who nearly got hurt along the way."

All their witnesses had taken risks to help them get to the Speaker. They'd pulled in a lot of favours and it was sheer luck that nothing had gone awry.

"I get that. But I'm still going to celebrate my extraordinary wife's amazing achievement."

Cameron stood to retrieve the Champagne he'd optimistically put in the fridge.

Michelle grabbed his T-shirt and pulled him back onto the couch.

"Thank you for your support on this one. Every time I got stuck you helped me work through it. I wouldn't have gotten to the motive without you."

"Stop trying to share the credit you earned on your own."

Cameron kissed her then pulled her off the couch and led her into the kitchen.

He popped the Champagne and Tessa cheered while Michelle took a bow. She was heartened her efforts were appreciated by the two people whose opinions she valued the most.

Cameron went to take a shower and Michelle propped herself up on the counter.

Tessa was frying vegetarian mince. "You look exhausted."

"I am exhausted. I'll eat an extra salad," Michelle promised, to alleviate her daughter's concerns.

"Are you glad it's over?"

"It's not over for us yet. We still have a lot of paperwork to do. But it's over for you. The media are done with the story now. There will be some other scandal tomorrow," Michelle hoped, though she suspected Tessa quietly enjoyed her new status.

Tessa laughed. "But you didn't find out who stole the mace."

Tessa seemed to be the only one who had noticed.

"No, but we got it back and sometimes that's more important," Michelle claimed diplomatically, not wanting to sound like she was condoning crime.

"Is it mutually exclusive?" Tessa asked, pretty sure it was better to do both.

Michelle wasn't in the mood to waste another second of precious time with her daughter discussing the mace.

"It doesn't matter. You're famous now, so some good has come of this saga after all," Michelle teased.

Tessa's phone rang and she took the pan off the stove and went outside to speak to her girlfriend.

Too tired to carry herself back to the couch, Michelle sat and shredded lettuce.

As the shards fell away, Michelle thought of Elizabeth who had died without knowing her husband was not sent to jail, who had stood up to a stranger invading her deathbed. The injustice sickened Michelle. She was still troubled by the lines she'd crossed.

Cameron returned to the kitchen and took over from Tessa who was still on the phone.

"Why are you crying into the lettuce?"

"I didn't realise," Michelle replied numbly.

"If you could start again and do anything differently, what would you change?" Cameron asked.

He knew what Michelle needed. Sometimes humanity disguised itself as regret.

Michelle struggled to recall all the twists and turns. But as she thought back through the revelations and setbacks she could see with hindsight it could only have been as it was.

"You know, now that I think about it, so many of our break-throughs were on the back of dead ends."

"Like what?"

"Well, we met the reverend through a fake tip and then he end-ed up helping us get the mace back. And we met Alfred before we figured out the motive, and he ended up giving us the statement that got us the warrant we needed. And I figured out the motive because you were joking about public relations stunts."

For a team who prided themselves on a disbelief in coinciden-ces, their case was riddled with them.

Cameron could see straight through her.

"Don't try and explain this away. You followed those leads and you put those pieces together. You solved the case because you're a brilliant detective and you would have got there regardless of how the chips fell."

"I missed the window," Michelle argued, enamoured by his re-fusal to accept she was fallible.

"And I once accidently cut down the wrong tree. We all make mistakes," Cameron replied. Like his love and pride, his support for his wife was unshakeable.

# 42

Chom didn't have a frivolous bone in his body but there was one ritual he condoned. The post case awards.

They were deadlocked.

"William Robinson is my least favourite and there is nothing you can say to change my mind," Michelle declared adamantly.

"But Fredrick Davis turned out to be one of the bad guys," Tamzyn demanded.

Michelle shook her head. "Chom, talk some sense into her."

Chom laughed. "Can we give least favourite to the media?"

"No!" Michelle and Tamzyn shouted in unison.

Michelle took a bite of her celebratory souvlaki.

"Sorry, Tamzyn. Fredrick was actually very polite and he was lovely to Susan Hadley. William Robinson it is. Please do the honours."

The honours consisted of writing the winner's name on the board.

Defeated, Tamzyn wrote 'William Robinson' on her freshly cleaned strategy board and added devil's horns and a tail.

They turned their minds to the favourite award.

Tamzyn stared, hands on her hips, at the archive boxes.

"This is going to be so hard, there were so many good ones."

"You've got ten minutes until your teleconference with the Governor," Chom reminded Tamzyn who was notoriously indecisive.

After their prolonged public evisceration and then redemption, the Governor had decided to award the detectives a Medal of Valour.

"You can't choose Annie. Friends are disqualified," Tamzyn said to Michelle.

Michelle rolled her eyes. "My gut's telling me George Pearse but I also have a soft spot for Mary Cousins."

"This isn't a bravery award," Tamzyn argued. Mary had been on her least favourite list.

Chom rescued Mary from a character assassination.

"How about Robert? Great attitude, works for free, super positive, perhaps a little naive but we can't all be jaded."

"Nice. I do like Robert," Michelle agreed.

"I do also like George," Chom replied.

Tamzyn deliberately steered clear of Thomas Jeffrey.

"I feel like the reverend and Alfred helped us solve the case, but Samuel was so soulful and Florrie was just this powerhouse of knowledge and wisdom."

Chom laughed. "You can't have four, Tamzyn."

"Okay, two. Samuel and Florrie," Tamzyn negotiated, airing her internal battle.

Michelle gave her partner a disapproving head shake.

"No, pick one."

"Florrie," Tamzyn committed and returned to the couch.

Michelle gasped and jumped out of her seat. "I forgot Vida.

I'm changing my vote."

Chom looked confused. "Who's Vida?"

"The window," Michelle reminded him.

"Sorry, Vida's not eligible for nomination. She's not in any of the reports so technically she's not connected to the case," Chom quashed, enforcing the rules of the game.

"Fine," Michelle conceded. "Still, cheers to Vida."

They raised their soft drink bottles.

"If we're open to going avant-garde. I think we should nominate the person who returned the mace." Tamzyn raised a finger. "Technically they're in the report, we just don't know who they are."

Michelle laughed. "They are definitely my favourite."

Chom smiled. "Why not? Tamzyn, do the honours."

Tamzyn triumphantly approached the board and wrote 'Person-Who-Returned-The-Mace' and then put a halo above it and surrounded the phrase with hearts.

"Great work, team. Happy for these to go out?" Chom pointed to the files and they both nodded.

He put his empty soft drink bottle on Tamzyn's desk and left to wheel the archive boxes down to the mail room to be couriered to the lawyers.

"Why are you smiling?" Michelle asked, in response to Tamzyn's cheeky grin.

Tamzyn sat back down next to Michelle.

"It's pretty funny we're getting an award for a case we didn't solve."

The reverend had been admonished by the media for refusing to give up the identity of the thief. It didn't seem to matter that he didn't know who it was.

Michelle pondered the irony. "Does it bother you we don't know who stole the mace?"

"Not in the slightest," Tamzyn replied contently. Normally the loose ends would be eating her alive. "It just feels… peaceful. Like a friendly ghost was helping us, or an angel."

Michelle laughed. Like her partner, she was just happy to be done with the mace mystery once and for all. But she was fairly sure she knew which human had stolen the mace, and an angel wasn't far off.

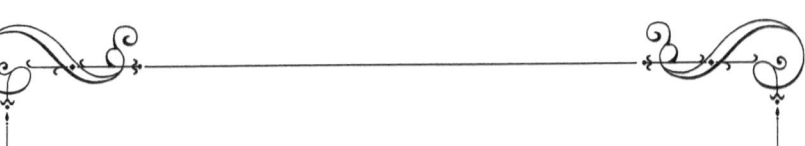

## *Lemons and Leaves*

My sisters and I stood, arms linked, on the back porch. Tears in our eyes and pain in our hearts, silently watching our mother say goodbye to her lemon tree. We knew this day would come. The house which was the only home we'd known until we were mothers ourselves had become needy. Too many rooms for one person who had in her own time conceded the house she had built, which tenderly held our memories, was now a shell. Outgrown by all who had once cherished its warmth.

I looked at my mother transfixed on this tree, which to any other eyes bore lemons and leaves, knowing which moments she was remembering. The countless pets buried under it, the children and grandchildren clambering over it, the images of our father rustling possums out of it with a broom. Any other lemon tree would not be covered in scars from swings and strings, the support to our adventures and the flavour to our celebrations.

While my sisters wept I walked the garden, not ready to leave for the last time. Each planter a family outing, each fence a superficial barrier. Flower beds where we spent weekends together on our knees, covered in dirt, laughing and playing and enjoying lazy afternoons together.

I relived our first summer. The house just built had smelt of paint, and construction of the new neighbourhood had provided a constant layer of dust over the manicured garden. Freshly installed, immature and fickle. Years of experiments and uprooting had culminated in the current arrangement. The lemon tree was the only survivor from the original landscape design. Robust and resilient, the longest serving resident of this home would remain for the next family to enjoy.

We had asked our mother whether she wanted to take the lemon tree to her new flat in the retirement village but she felt the tree would be wasted on her alone. She preferred that the next family have the pleasure of its company. Watching her now, I wanted to beg her to keep it but I knew it was really me who didn't want to part with this integral fixture from my childhood. Our father, our house and now our lemon tree. It seemed too much but my mother understood it was not the tree we missed. She reached up and patted the lowest branch, whispering her thanks for its fruit and shelter. One sister broke away from their embrace to gather the last of the lemons.

I checked the rooms for stray trinkets we may have missed. Boxes lined the walls. The furniture had been wrapped, ready to be relocated or donated. The delicate heirlooms were in my car to be carefully transported with the devotion they deserved. Stripped bare, the house revealed its tiredness. Hidden carpet stains exposed, cracks illuminated against the emptiness. The fullness of our family life had left its mark on every surface.

My sisters ushered our mother to the car while I locked the front door for the final time. No one bothered to try and hold back tears. Devastated neighbours stood on their porches, braced for our departure. Goodbyes had been said in intimate settings over the preceding months and weeks. Late into the night my mother and her contemporaries reminisced over the children they had raised and the lives they had led from this little street. Decades of stories to decanter and repackage, reviving the outrageous and dwelling on the momentous. The process of honouring a home in a street of homes readying to be reincarnated. An extended family behind every door. A friend keeping watch at every window.

Before driving away we looked back on the building which was no longer ours, in the street where we no longer lived, and contemplated how lucky we'd been. My mother sat beside me with a basket of lemons on her lap and a shiny new key in her hand. She turned to me and smiled and told me she was ready to go home.

## Other Titles from Emma Adair

*2068*
*Four Chambers*